Praise for ~

Acacia

a book of wonders

The tangle of nervous systems and fever dreams that pulse within *Acacia* reminds me of an old hymn dipped in technicolor and then broadcast through the speakers of a two-toned Lincoln Continental. Church is where you make it. Shall we gather within the ruination to practice resurrection? *Acacia* suggests that if we do, we might experience salvation on terms we never imagined. Vincent James has written a mesmerizing novel teeming with gorgeous sentences. It's the sort of remarkable book that manufactures its own uncanny light by which to read.

—**Selah Saterstrom,** author of
Ideal Suggestions
& Rancher

Acacia, by Vincent James, is exactly what it claims to be, *a book of wonders.* Strange, moving, extraordinary, this is work built with serious brio and serious craft. James can spin a fabulous yarn *and* he can write a hell of a sentence: it doesn't get any better than that.

—**Laird Hunt,** author of *Zorrie*
& This Wide
Terraqueous World

More Praise ~

Acacia is an incantatory and perilous epic about lostness, about fear, about worlding outwards against the confines of treacherous boundaries. James's lush language feels like a series of invocations, the reaching and desire described in the words, resonant and enacted by the gathering of energies, by the novel's own visionary musicality. As I read, I can feel these words wanting to be recited, caught in my throat like spells. This book is magical and a revelation.

—**Janice Lee,** author of
Separation Anxiety
& Imagine a Death

Acacia, *a book of wonders*

Acacia

a book of wonders

a novel by

Vincent James

★trp
the university press of shsu
huntsville · texas
www.texasreviewpress.org

Library of Congress Cataloging-in-Publication Data
Names: James, Vincent (Fiction author), author.
Title: Acacia, a book of wonders: a novel / Vincent James.
Description: First edition. | Huntsville: TRP: The University Press of SHSU
Identifiers: LCCN 2022022415 (print) | LCCN 2022022416 | (ebook) | ISBN
   9781680032987 (paperback) | ISBN 9781680032994 (ebook)
Subjects: LCSH: Matriarchal Cults—Texas, East—Fiction. | Historical—
   Fiction. Forest gods—Fiction. | Arkansas—Fiction. | LCGFT: Novels. |
   Fantasy fiction.
Classification: LCC PS3610.A4596 A64 2023 (print)
   LCC PS3610.A4596 | (ebook) | DDC 813/.6—dc23/eng/20220513
   LC record available at https://lccn.loc.gov/2022022415
   LC ebook record available at https://lccn.loc.gov/2022022416
FIRST EDITION
Cover collage courtesy of Vincent James
Author photo courtesy: Laird Hunt
Printed and bound in the United States of America
The University Press of SHSU
Huntsville, Texas 77341
texasreviewpress.org

For the Solitaires

Contents

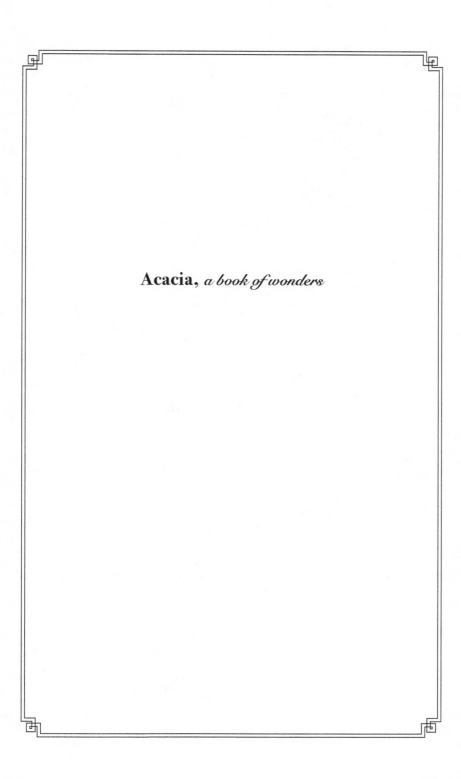

Acacia, *a book of wonders*

EAST TEXAS, LATE 1980s. In the eastern part of Texas, nearby the Lake O' The Pines, dawn fog hazes the thicket. Troubles its dense and prickled girth. Loblolly branches entangle gray dripping moss, the glistening hair of Absalom. An abandoned lumber mill rises from the innards of the bramble, its signage sun-bleached of the company name.

Prior decades beat the thicket back. Established structure and domain. But that ground is lost now, and the mill long overtaken, and the sandy hillocks of fire ants surround. The thicket advances at the speed of springs, summers, and the loose foliage subsumed in its mass, steadily, silently, toward a two-lane road.

East Texas stillness, broken by engine whine and smoke. A dirtbike bursts from the thicket, sliding on bald tires among the chaparral. The rider downshifts, heading for a nearby levee; then for the country lane; then for a town twenty miles hence.

The rider is a naked boy. An iron collar is fastened about his neck. From the collar, a long length of dull chain extends to the sky. There, a like collar binds the boy to a red-faced vulture. On ash-black wings, the bird wheels the currents, hissing, panting.

THE *Meditations* OF *Petra Caldwell* CONTAINING *the* TRUE ACCOUNT *of* ACACIA & HER CAPTIVITY THEREIN, AS WRITTEN *in* HER LITTLE BOOKS

Dear Reader,

It was said of the Prophetess Mother Salome Nightingale that when her back tooth abscessed and was extracted the hole arrived already sutured and nary a drop of ruby blood presented.

It was said that once the Prophetess Mother laid her body across a child, drowned on a feast day in the northside well, and that she pressed her mouth to its bloated purple lips, and that when she prayed to the bird the child returned from the deep. It was said that when she lit her tobacco pipe after breakfast from her oxblood velvet chair at the head of Acacia's table, she could store the elegant, long-stemmed Churchwarden under her arm for any duration of time she wished—and that when she returned it to her mouth at her own good pleasure, the embers remained lit and ready for her draw. Her blessing commuted the brand of otherworldly confidence that turned a quivering Saul of Tarsus into the crusading Apostle Paul, this was said too.

It was often said, indeed it was celebrated, that her face did not age; that her hair did not grey; that no matter her labors in Acacia's garden or chapel, her vigor redoubled upon itself like a sturdy, coiled cord. It was said that the terrors of the world coursed through her in sleep, that the awe of genocide and the child's white lie sieved through her vessel, and that she worked out their Heavenly purposes in the liminal jurisdiction of slumber, and it was said that when she returned each morning from an eventide of worldly ailments, she offered the most potent theodicies of Heaven's justification.

It was said of her that with her cream muslin dress hiked and knotted at the thigh and wearing a pair of worn running shoes, that she and her son could outrun the youngest men of Acacia in a three-legged race, and that she could quote *Willy Wonka and the Chocolate Factory* from memory after a single VHS screening on the television in her bedroom, and that she kept an encyclopedia of magic tricks under her nightstand so that she could continually improve upon her cardcraft for the wonderment of Acacia's children.

My curious Reader, it has been said many silly things.

Enclosed is the true account of Acacia, and of one innocent's captivity in the Prophetess Mother Salome Nightingale's wooden sheds. It is the compendium of my life, written in my precious little books—an archive I believed lost throughout the course of my many mortifications, or seized by the Nightingale, who taunted they'd been burned. But like the amercements of Nebuchadnezzar, my writings were preserved by a power greater than I, and for such a time as this, and the Mother's flames did not destroy my pages but only illumined their substance. I have assembled these pages in-kind with great attentiveness, reconstructing them when necessary while also inscribing seventeen complementary reflections for you, dear Reader, all that I might wrench my legacy from the hands of mythmakers, slanderers, and workers of aspersion; all that I might make the crooked paths straight.

Reader, soothe this true account. Pet it like a hackled haunch. For in these writings in my little books I often present a mind harrowed, undone, and bent in scoliosis. But reader, I want you to feel what I did in all my bewilderment and apocrypha, and so I ask you to imagine yourself as me, as Petra Caldwell, a spirited seventeen-year-old girl banished, nay *escaped*, from the dominion of her father's strange fervors only to emerge for the worse as the captive of a brutal materfamilias. And so I implore you to straighten me out. Even now as you read—witnessing my growing affections for the Nightingale's Son, absorbing my efforts at escape, appreciating the immense weight of Heaven's ordination—you may divine the conclusion. Let the Reader read.

Within the matrices of Heaven, and a reader myself of its mysteries, still, and faithfully,

~ *Petra Caldwell*

BOOK I

THE FERVOR *of the* PATRIARCH
& A HEART *of* STONE
& RENDERED *to the* FLAMES
& THE GREAT IRON HORSE
& THE VULTURE,
a HEAVENLY GUIDE
& A CITY *of* JUBILEE
& THE NIGHTINGALE *and* HER SON
& A FAITHFUL SERVANT

I was born Petra Caldwell to a mother and father of precepts. Precepts revealed to my father as a young man through a certain, hidden sensitivity of his spirit. Our home was a self-sustained farm in Arkansas. Father's aptitude was soft red wheat. I wished for a sister in a little white dress. I wished for a cut of good bloody chuck. I will return to the sister. I will return to the meat.

It was 1971, and the Caldwell farm flourished enough. And yet, behold my father, grimed from his labor in the fields, tyrannous at the head of our humble, ruby Formica table. He gripped a burnished handbell in one heavy, chapped hand. Swallowed up in his other palm were a pair of six-sided dice. His leather book, which never left his sight, lay open on the table before us. Mother had set our table with a pauper's banquet — a runt loaf of spelt and flaxseed. This was all we were permitted.

Father fondled the worn handle of his bell. When it rang, it meant recite.

Ring.

Father uttered his scripture first, a long and familiar passage from his book. His diligence burned like a cattle brand. His flawless tour of the words, as rhythmic and incantatory as a coxswain singing to the rowers, purchased his reward—an abundant portion of the daily bread. Mother slicked it with a glob of butter from her dull pewter knife. As Father ate, he released the dice and turned his book to the precepts they dictated.

Ring.

Mother's recitation came next. She stuttered on a *thee* or a *thou*, for Ava Caldwell practiced Heaven's demands with half a heart and even less a voice. A smaller slice due her. She chewed the bread slowly, as if savoring a cherry cordial. Father threw again and turned his intent on me.

Ring.

Ring.

Ring.

My recitation was silence. My silence was the end of days. For as of late, I had grown prodigal—dog-hearted—mutinous, and ever more prone to the strange dreams and trances I had suffered since I was a young girl. Because one rotting peach in the fruit bowl putrefies the bounty which surrounds it—because a claret ink blot bleeds in the wash and soils the whites—because rebellion is as grand an offense as witchcraft—my father cast me out. But not before I got ahold of his book. I held it by the black leather cover to the flaming mouth of our cookstove and watched my patriarchate dissolve like snow in spring thaw.

Ring, I said.

At my insistence, he rolled the dice, and I burned the page they dictated.

Ring, I said.

Another page toward the back. This one I tore out and stored in the bib of my pinstripe overalls—an uncanny map of sorts with intricate mazework, marked by the yearly dates of his many failed attempts at its solution.

Ring. Ring. Ring.

His book went to the flames. And I shook off the dust of my father's house.

Seventeen, and just shy my GED from the nearby town of Jesper's only high school, I wandered.

I found my pardon on the trains, with my kin of the boxcars, and my hair matted, and I shored-up the holes in my shoes with scraps of cardboard.

From the railways, I saw apple orchards burst abundant, and nymph shadows flitting through the forests, and low-tide oceans giving of their treasures, and deserts still and haunted, and smugglers' tunnels along the borders, and streams babbling with the language of the dead. I nourished on cans of tuna and drank Boone's Farm strawberry wine and kept a sleep-grip on my shank should a fellow drifter mark me for his beau.

Around my nineteenth birthday, which arrives in July when the fireworks have passed and all of Jesper sit on their hands until football season, I had completed a grand circuit of the railways from coast to coast and felt myself compelled by opportunity, or will, or perhaps by the dreams in which I walked the mazework of my father's careful scrawl back toward the landscape of my origin.

And so, on a morning with the East Texas air thick as gruel, I spotted a sign for a lumber mill and shortly after rolled out of a boxcar and into a rural trainyard. It was just shy of dawn. I bet on the cover of darkness and stepped into the quad, sniffing for the railyard bulls. And verily, I had not made it two sure steps before a holler and a pistol shot set me scrambling.

Even in the silty morning dim, I could make out the law on the catwalk of a nearby control tower. He gave chase, wheeling his bulk between the metal scaffolding and around the tight turns of the exterior staircase like a crackerjack square dancer. I had a small lead, but little knowledge of my vicinities. Surrendering the cover of the train cars, I bolted for a nearby treeline and pushed deep into the brush. Thorns tugged at my baggy overalls and snarled up my dark curls like all creation had convened to keep me captive. Desperate, I sawed off a healthy sprout with my shiv and was free for the moment, though none the prettier for the lopsided updo I now surely wore upon my skull.

The bull's curses soon faded, then disappeared entirely. I took a slower pace and let my breath settle down and hiked for an indeterminate amount of time, thinking I might break through to the other side of the trees eventually and find and follow the tracks to some small rail town. All the while, I appreciated the span of eerie woods I found myself in. Thick and mature, the verdant forest was frothy with moss, and showed no reveal of recent human trespass. So occupied, my boot caught in a grip of roots as I crossed through a burbling creek and I sprawled face-first into a waist-high tower of smooth, stacked river rocks, toppling some old hiker's mound to chart their path.

Long throbbing moments I spent soaking there, dizzied, anxious, and thoroughly worn-through.

When at last I sat up, I appreciated a change in the water surrounding me. As if a flash flood had engorged the streamlet, hazy eddies now churned and dispelled around my shins and bottom like the ephemeral language of angels.

I tended to my face with my mother's red handkerchief, which I wore always tied around my neck, wiping bloodlets from my forehead, and off my eyelashes, and from the tip of my nose and my crooked upper lip, but the wounds still ran and splat blood into the water's seething surface to instantly disseminate.

On a sudden, sharp whispers cut across the forest in a language unfamiliar. I waited in silence as the strange words spread throughout my consciousness like sheet lightning rips through clouds—*Hortus conclusus. Hortus conclusus. Hortus conclusus.*

Unsteady as I was, I found my feet and sought the sender.

The chants were not issued by the pursuing bull, nor by a grimy chum from the train who had followed me in and wished to give me a scare. No rescuer; no small boy squirrel hunting. The only living creature I did spy was a large bird, a vulture, standing on the ground on the other side of the crick. I thought it must be injured as I, but the bird cocked its cruor head and unfurled its wings with majesty, and the ombre, ashy-white feathers of its undercarriage bristled in the breeze.

The whisper again: *hortus conclusus.*

I rose and made my way toward the bird. It allowed me to draw close, close enough I fancied I might touch it, like a tamed animal at a petting zoo. I reached my bloodied palm to its hairless skull. The bird then leapt, and with a deft flap of its wings landed further in the woods, and I hobbled after it into thicker foliage, across freshly made animal tracks. When I felt dizzy and paused to rest, the bird yawped at me and feinted a charge, and I feared disappointing its peculiar summons would mean the rend of its beak.

In time, our wildering tour of the woods returned us to the crick and behold — the mound of hiker's rocks stood restacked as before. I touched my forehead, and the wound those stones had delivered me remained fresh, dribbling heavy blood like the thick drool of my father's old bloodhound. I listened for the sounds of the train, for some silver thread leading back to their familiar tracks, but only silence presented.

Meanwhile, the bird waited for me ahead in the water, plucking at something rotting: the ribcage and fur of a half-butchered fox. The dead animal's mangled coat was a muted gold, and its head topped with expansive rounded ears, and its legs were long and muscular as a Boxer dog's. The bird hurried on as I reached the carcass, and I did forge after it as my guide in this beguilement, I did, but not before kneeling at the glimmer of something in the abnormal creature's split stomach.

The object was a small leather strop, like a keychain one fastens around their belt loop. It was dented, and worn, and emblazoned with a handsome gold-buttoned closure, remarkably attractive. I thought of the beaucoup bucks it might fetch in hock, of all the cans of tuna such a prize could buy, and I picked it from the bloodied carcass with two fingers like a child tweezes a bone in the game of *Operation*. I then rinsed the object in the stream, buffed it dry on my sleeve, and took a closer look. The gold totem bore the shape of a compass and was crudely tooled on the back of its thick, leather band with the initials of its prior owner — "E. Muir." I pocketed it in my overalls next to my father's maze and renewed my tail of the bird, possessed for the moment by what other treasures it might soon pass me by.

The landscape twisted around us. The sun had not moved. Another pass through the crick, and I could not find the original path that had brought us this far. In this return, the foxlike creature was gone, and the stones glistened with rich, fresh moss, and the water was shallower but whisked around my ankles like a roiling pot. I followed the bird as we transgressed new, denser terrain. Between the wild eruptions of blackjack oak, thick convolutions of menacing briar overlapped upon themselves well above my height, like a dozen layers of concertina wire. And then I was submerged to my waist in blackwater swamp. I lost my backpack, bedroll, and shank in that morass, surrounded by pink and green pitcher plants and the peering yellow eyes of the stealthful creatures of that place.

Thus, transformed from a modestly greased roamer into the soiled visage of a skunk ape, in time I reached terra firma and muscled past the final defense of bramble, which did catch my cheek afresh with one clawing thorn.

With the bird just before me, I stumbled at last into a clearing of curious ordination. Heaven and its raptor had shepherded me to Acacia.

Before me, like the stations of a clock, twelve wooden sheds circled a wide oval perimeter, perhaps half a mile in diameter, sprinkled here and there with a small population of men working the grounds.

Against the treeline on the right side stood a chapel, complete with a charming, pear-green, wooden-shingled steeple. A small well, encircled by white stones, sat next to the chapel, and another larger version of the well was built closer to the clearing's center. Across the clearing, on the left flank of the territory, stood a grand two-story estate, built of gorgeous blond timber that had weathered over time to a soothing, muted green. The structure's walls crawled with the tendrils of a wild vine that snaked around a series of glorious six-foot windows, opened wide to the humid evening air. Lace curtains billowed forth from these windows like the regimental advance of a ghostly militia. The barrier of bramble I had just emerged from circled around the entire clearing and guarded the estate's rear.

As I considered this rural seat, the front door of the residence opened. What strange Elysium. A line of women, arranged from the elderly to their early teens, and dressed alike in cream muslin dresses or stovepipe pants with matching muslin tops, promenaded in single file from the house like a serpent exiting its burrow. Each woman carried a large glass jar in which burned a thin, silvery candle. Descending the porch stairs, they threaded their way through the bountiful garden rows abutting the estate, each stepping in the woman ahead's footfall, as if to treat the soil reverently. All the while they murmured some urgent prayer. As they passed betwixt the number of men finishing their work in the garden, the men took pause, and as if receiving a blessing, each lifted the crude tool he carried—a kind of rake, with a stock of thick live oak, nearly four-feet in length, and topped with a head of dull grimacing iron, forged with thick conal studs.

My wonderment was multiplied when a voice called out — *Petra* — my name.

From the door of the estate, a woman now beckoned. She was barefoot, short of five-feet tall, and her hair was bound into a cinnabar-colored topknot. She wore a long dress of bleached sackcloth, tied at the waist, with wide bell sleeves. I obeyed her summons with some wariness, keen on the procession and the men with the rakes as I passed them by, but they only eyed me with a striking countenance, so assured. As I drew closer, the woman on the porch made a sign with her hand — a curving swoop across her chest with her palm straight and rigid and bent upwards at the wrist. A large silver wristwatch slid up the length of her bony arm and then back to the slight fluttering of her fingers. I took some concern after the bottoms of her bare feet, for rather than stepping, she flagellated them across the splintered boards of the porch. Though she was small and wore little adornment, I had no misgivings — she was the dowager of this place; a sovereign who by some magic knew me by name.

Behind her, a man joined. He looked to be a few years older than me, and was handsome, with long, mercury-colored hair and a strong dimpled chin. He introduced her — The Prophetess Mother Salome Nightingale — and then himself as simply, her Son.

The men with rakes ceased their work. Joined by the women with the candles, they congregated in the yard behind me in a half moon. By my quick guesswork, they numbered nearly eighty souls. The Nightingale and the Son then ushered me inside the Pear House, the name of this grand estate, shutting the door behind us as a sweet song commenced from the gathering outside; a soothing melody. The song gently suggested itself as "Moon River," though the emphasis on certain syllables lasted too long and the singers held the melody like a sleepy driver drifting off the road. Beyond this, the lyrics were warped, wrangled instead into an eccentric ode to this place.

At the threshold, the Pear House revealed an immense open foyer. Large throw rugs covered the slate floor. Low-set divans and supple leather colonial chairs littered the space in small groupings. An imposing walnut bookshelf sat against the back wall immediately opposite me, and on comfortable shearling throw rugs, small children silently absorbed themselves while a man with a kindly air oversaw their study. Next to the library, a single staircase led to the upper floor.

The Son of the Nightingale ushered me to the right-hand side of this grand room, toward an exceedingly long table with an antique lace tablecloth and a striking centerpiece of wildflowers, braided thistles, and all manner of feathers. Long bench seats lined each side of the table. Completing the tableau, a colossal ox-blood velvet chair sat at the head.

The Nightingale took this seat of honor and motioned me toward the bench with no apparent care to the layers of mud-died mess I carried on my person. No sooner had I seated myself than another woman entered from the arched doorway behind her. She was very young, with vibrant, dewy skin and limber arms, and her hair was bound upward as the Prophetess's, and she wore a frilled white apron tied around her waist. She carried a tray and, atop it, a porcelain bowl; a bowl so delicate and ornate it should only sit within a museum's glass case to be admired. She set it before me, and I have never known such a stripe of hunger as I did in that moment—the hunger of profound mystification. With a permissive nod from the Nightingale, I descended upon the cubed meat and the jeweled root vegetables that surrounded it as a youngster does their Christmas bounty.

The Nightingale drew her bare feet beneath her and lit a pipe, a straight-stemmed Dr. Grabow Lark, the kind I'd seen sequestered behind the register at the Walgreens in Little Rock. Casting quick glances, I perceived that the eyes in her skull resembled those of the bird in the thicket. Perhaps she saw the same in mine. The wound on my head tingled afresh and my crooked lip did also quiver with dread and fascination. Though she refrained from querying me — and I her — much silently passed between us in that time.

When I had finished my bowl, and it had been refilled by Fleur, the maiden of the kitchen, and I had finished that second helping likewise, the Nightingale suggested the Son show me to my quarters. Passing by the children, the Son led me up the staircase to a simply furnished room immediately at its crest. Desire and worry and hesitation were displaced in an instant by the sight of that inviting brass bed, the pillowy comforter atop it, and I shed my boots and ruined overalls and stripped off my undershirt to a nearby laundry hamper, and having bathed myself with washcloths and a basin of water left for me, lay myself down upon the linens to immediately pass the ensuing hours in a dreamless sleep.

The following morning the Nightingale woke me in my room. My garments were gone, and with them, stored in the pocket of the overalls, my father's page of mazework and the golden bauble from the fox's carriage. The Mother carried a cream dress on a wooden hanger and a pair of second-hand New Balances.

Dressing me, she gave me my tasks for the day in short military order: gathering berries, scrubbing a hamper of coarse garments in a nearby inlet of water, followed by a time of meditation in the chapel, all to be accomplished by mid-afternoon. Not a word of her knowledge of my name did she afford me, nor of my arrival into this, their sacred grove. Seemingly briefed by some divinity, she adopted me wholesale—my lip prone to temper, my leeriness of ritual, the kiss across my forehead from the thicket's stone, and all. For myself, I resolved to explore the marvelous boon of this shelter without risking the offense my brimming curiosity might incur.

And to my tasks, I applied myself with a diligence even my father would have rewarded, perhaps with a full-portion of butter. For two lost years I had bounded the rails; sought small miracles; fought off rapine hands with the stab of my shank; once, nibbled the transcendent puff of a Three Musketeers when hungry as many days; hit the jackpot — thick trousers, a leather belt, and a Pendleton blanket — in a grocer's unlocked dumpster during the Minnesota winter. All of these indicated Heaven's tending. Still, it took Acacia; took their swarm of love and tenderness that fit me into their flock like a winning Tetris piece to settle my seeking spirit.

But my jubilation was short-lived. For even as I affected sincere worship in these early years, my life was transgression to the Prophetess Mother Salome Nightingale.

BOOK II

THICKET DALLIANCES
& A GLIMPSE of the CITY
in the CLOUDS
& THE BLUE TRUCK of ACACIA
& THE NIGHTINGALE'S TONGUE

It had been a sweet and sticky summer, and the Son and I saw fit for secret swimming. We had a hidden place, when the Nightingale was away on errands outside the thicket and the labor was lax, where we could steal away — a watery respite drawn from the nearby Lake O' The Pines, choked by catch-weed and thin to a drip at some inclines, then coursing as the rapids in others, which ultimately fed into our grove of deep water. Leaves and branches bearing gooseberries canopied the banks, ornamentally lit and reflected in the water, as if staged for a play. As the year had drawn on and the Son and I grew fond of each other, we made this place our own private kingdom.

On this day, lust smoked off the Son. He splashed like an otter, then floated on his back, tempting me with his sex. He found a beachball that had survived its journey from the merrymakers at the Lake O' The Pines and batted it my way. I saw him, yes, all of him, and while typically I'd have leapt to his coquetry, a grander site arrested me.

The surface of the water has turned. It moves like the slow churn of lava. The foliage around us looks caught in flame, leisurely aflutter, the color deeply saturated. But even more, the sublime site above: the outline of an ash-grey palace rises from the low-lying clouds. It is mighty, heavily mortared, and many towered, and surrounded by curtain walls and fortified parapets. Candlelight flutters behind the diamond-shaped windows cut into its towers, and birds, so many birds, make their circuit from window to window, like doctors tending to their charges. From air to moat to the grand staircase leading to a celestial keep, bright jeweled blurs descend and ascend the stronghold as if reinforcing the battlements. Human likenesses of the Acacians I know, and many more besides whom I don't, flicker beneath their glow.

Does the Son see such wonder? You would ask, but he has dove back under water. And this is why — the men with rakes wait on the bank — we have been found.

The Mother punished me with labor in the chapel despite the day of rest. Under the watchful eye of our candlework, I did tend the benches with linseed oil and all the while prayed, as I was instructed, for the solvency of my soul and a rootedness of my heart toward Acacia. And yet, with those long hours alone, with my lip agitated of its own accord, I returned like a moth captivated by porch light to the magnificence I had witnessed above the water, soaring among these birds to peer into the keep's windows, where I spied only the still expanse of the void and those mysteries yet to be revealed to me.

That glory, yes, but there was also the diversion of the Son. The Mother's interventions burned like sparklers in the dark, but his sunshine fizzled their potency. I wondered again at what harm a stirring for the Son could actually accomplish, for such a thing felt as fine and natural to me as the devotion I dually carried for the Prophetess Mother. Peering in through the chapel window at me, he waved and blew to me a kiss. I did then catch that airborne Valentine, and in the place most sacred to our worship, set it resolvedly to my lips. The inlet would not be the last time we were found.

Years before I arrived in Acacia, a saint was deep in Acacia's thicket returning from one of the Mother's sacred errands. Skittering on a cleared sideroad he lost control of our beat-up relic of a blue pickup truck and went down a decline, caving it in against a dead tree. Extraction impossible, the truck was abandoned.

Since then, the chassis demoralized. Field mice chanced the carburetor and gnawed the wiring, storing their seeds about the engine's crevices. The bench-seat sheltered a family of foxes, wintering in the upholstery.

The Son and I sprawled out on quilts in the bed of the truck when we could safely sneak away under the cover of darkness, our feet jutting off the back end, for the bed was small, and on this night we were good and drunk on suntea jars of fermented fruit: ceremonial Acacian wine. The Son tucked my hair behind the ear to cradle my face, tracing a finger along the curve of my lip. I watched his eyes drift and close, and he slept in the bow of my arm. We were prodigious lovers before sunrise.

And so, I dressed; dawn was near, and if spotted, it might appear I was only out for an early walk, was not an indulgent of the fruit the Mother had forbidden.

I knew the gnarl of the dark greenery returning to Acacia's clearing; the long, slow growth of its trees. I knew this bramble and what it hid: each structure, old encampment, and ancient haunt. I'd uncovered bleached cans of empty Schlitz (while gathering berries in these woods) and discarded prison uniforms, human bones, and even a bag of moldy money. I knew these woods. I had time before Acacia woke. Ahead, a split in the path rounded a bend. Wild boars watched my movements.

I recalled for reason unknown an August Saturday at my family's farm when my father was away. I had a bowl of cold cereal balanced on the tight pull of the nightgown stretched across my knees as I watched *Underdog* on our small television. The heroic puppy misunderstood such vast amounts of the criminal's grand plans, but such was his power, and the power of his love for Sweet Polly Purebred, that he crashed through walls and water towers and bank vaults and mountains until every hulking foe lay unconscious, contorted, and hog-tied with black X's for eyes.

Beyond the next group of boulders, past the most majestic loblolly pine in our thicket, should be the Pear House. But rounding the path I found the geography of the thicket had misled me. For I had returned to the recognizable decline off the beaten path, and there, through the crush of foliage that never tangled back, rested the carcass of Acacia's blue truck.

I treaded toward it. The blanket was spread as before. The Son still slumbered. I had watched him this way many times in our nighttime dalliances. How he dreamed; how he murmured.

I felt a curious tranquility settle over me, and my lip did again twitch. How much his face now resembled the face of the Mother. Her hair, dark, his, shadowed. The inheritance of the Nightingale's sweeping eyelashes; the Elvis-curl of her upper lip. His body, hers. The body, an amalgam of them both.

Slim shouldered, the body thrashed about the blanket as if puppeteered. Lips parted for teeth, beautifully set in the mouth, bright as klieg lights. Behind them, the tongue. I knew this organ; a wonderful wet thing that had slipped the canal of my ear, darted in my mouth, in my castle.

Jaws opened and expanded. A tongue trekked from the mouth, probing the air, curling, coiling. Extending too far, the tongue flopped against the face of the body with the collapse of a seductive cat. I thought it dead. I reached a hand for the familiarity of face—the Son's, the Mother's. But the tongue animated its will and struck against the palm of my hand. Its spittle burned like quicklime. The weed roots of my veins lit with her venom.

The Mother's eyes, everywhere at once. I had been found.

BOOK III

A FIRST CAPTIVITY in my WOODEN SHEDS & THE LITTLE BOOKS

That night after supper, when had I retired to my room in the Pear House, I was set upon by the men with rakes. A dozen hauled me up and aggressed me, though I was not ravished. My huckleberry friends removed me from the Pear House with as much sensitivity as a bouncer handles the town drunk. The Nightingale waited for me on the steps outside, surrounded by the women and their candles. Her countenance was vicious, her lips set with a sharp sneer, an affixment I had not seen in the time preceding. I may as well have pleaded mercy from a tempest. In only my nightclothes, she ordered me carried to one of the twelve small buildings on the perimeter of Acacia. I was thrown to the dirt floor, and the door was latched and padlocked.

The first of my wooden sheds.

I worried my fingernails, chewed them to the nubs. This must be some necessary initiation from the good saints of Acacia. Had I not proved my dedication? Had I not been faithful, with but few infringements generated from a sincere and titillated heart? I had laid my woven wreaths before the bird statue in the chapel. I had received the teachings of the Nightingale with tremor and weeping, and I had sung our hymns with heavenly contrition. I had opened my mouth to prophesy when the Mother had asked me to, and my words had edified; she herself lauded them. I had been pure in labor, foraging berries in the nearby thicket and had cared aptly for our garments. I had not degenerated. I had only fallen in love. I again placed my trust in the Nightingale. If my mettle must be tested through the fires of the Mother's furnace, so be it. When my devotion proved afresh, I would surely be welcomed back to our table.

These were my absurdities.

Days turned into weeks. My rations lessened; first food, then water. I was surveilled by the Nightingale through the gaps in the shed's walls; by her fowl eyes, feathered lashes, and by the rest of the Acacians likewise — the children, who surrounded my shed to peer-in on their object lesson, Petra the Wretched — the men with rakes, who took their rest from labor to mark my agonies — the women, who appeared at any hour of the night, announced only by the dim flicker of their candles. By Acacians, who had grown so dear to me over our time together — Tomsen, Esmerelda, Johannes, Wanda, and so many more wounding attendees besides.

Not a one would acknowledge my voice; my appeals. And only once was I given reprieve. Waking one morning, I found some-one had left the vessel for my account — several small, empty notebooks and black pens, hastily covered in dirt, in the corner of my shed.

My precious little books, with their black covers and wide-ruled pages, sold at the Piggly Wiggly or on the carousel displays at Walgreens. Less than a dollar apiece. Meant for the pocket. Meant for a prophetess.

BOOK IV

THE WRETCHED ESCAPES HER SHED
& A HUNTER DOES TREAD
& THE SEED of THOUGHTFUL REVENGE
& LIGHTNING and the TREES
& THE BLOSSOMS on HER BODY
& A MURMURATION of NAILS
& ANOTHER REMOVE
& THE WATCHING NIGHTINGALE

A piercing whistle—an approaching train on its rounds somewhere outside the thicket. I had waited all night for this summons, while Acacia slumbered, alone in my shed. When the whistle sounded again, louder, closer, I gave my all and charged, splatting my brittled constitution against the door. Again, again, throughout the shrilling coverage of the sound. Providence. On the fifth lunge, the old hinges burst.

Escape.

Through the planted gardens, into the thicket, across mud and water, under the moonlight, I chased after the train's thrumming chug. Above me, the camouflage of darkness cracked—soon there would be sun. My eyes were shark-cut; my thoughts lawless.

Slow, train. Please slow. Slow for Petra the Stowaway.

From the Pear House, the Nightingale's bellows sounded throughout the thicket and did seize my heart:

—Find Petra!

I plunged deeper into the woods. Dawn threatened my escape. I thought of myself as an actor on a stage, suddenly spotlit by the merciless morning blush of Heaven. Somewhere out here must tread a friendly hunter, after alligator and gray fox. Rations would fill his pack. A full canteen on his belt. A golden star guiding.

Breaking through to nearly the outer reach of the thicket, I spied a centipede of boxcars rolling across the flatlands. I darted toward the caboose, the very terminus of bramble reaching around my ankles.

Slow, train, please slow. Slow you fucking thing for Petra the Stowaway.

But the cruel, cold train did not slow for these reaching hands.

Fear churned my innards like I'd swallowed Prickly Pear. I receded back into the thicket to shield myself from the men with rakes, or chance upon the hunter and plead his help.

A hunter *did* stalk there. But he was the Son of the Nightingale. I was his trophy, his alligator, his thicket fox. I saw him first. I silenced my heartbeat, my ancient hinges, praying for escape. But keen, he spied me, face down, hiding in a holiday of mud.

The Son carried me back to Acacia, to the place of death lasting before and after, where the woman called The Prophetess Mother Salome Nightingale awaited, her head plenty bestrewn with ash. The Son laid me at her feet. I knew a little of her echoes, but my ear picked out a mind-bleaching whistle.

Had I lasted a scant thirty minutes longer in the sweet release of the thicket, I'd have caught another passing train. In the empowering span of this train's piping, I summoned my courage and rose to my feet before the Mother.

—I am Godbreath, Archangel of Heaven.
> *[See how the Nightingale curls like a*
> *trembling wisp before my virtue?]*

... Strip her.
> *[See how her body resists the calling*
> *of my regency? Her lumpy bones*
> *tumble about and strain her hoary*
> *skin, like a rover's kerchief bindle*
> *filled with canned goods.]*

... Shackle her to a whipping post in the great room of the Pear House.
> *[I beckon the curious children closer*
> *to prod her with arrowheads.]*

. . . The old adder Salome has been defanged.
> *[But alas, when all trains hush—*
> *my fantasias hush too—*
> *The Nightingale yet holds dominion.*
> *And I am not the Archangel*
> *Godbreath, but Petra the Wretched,*
> *nudist of the thicket, lesson for*
> *the children, and I have been*
> *imprisoned in a new shed, tucked*
> *under the largest trees*
> *in the compound.]*

Attempted flight had returned a bitterer punishment—a thick chain looped around my neck was padlocked to a crude, barred skylight in this shed's roof. My little books lost, left behind in the rush. In the corner of my new prison, I spied a glinting scrap of half-buried silver. It had my mind conceiving all kinds of treasures—a trowel, a key, a switchblade, a compass. But with my good arm, I unearthed only the faded wrapper of a candy bar.

I peered out of the holes in the porous timber. The grounds of Acacia appeared razed and smoldering. Smoke choked air. Ash grey pine needles blanketed earth. The Nightingale often made mention of the Commotions when she returned from her nightly prayer walks about the grounds—a grand and final advent of Heaven when the outside world sundered and fell to apocalypse, and family annihilated itself, and blood ran to the bridle. Acacia was the only safe citadel in this doomsday—this she swore. But perhaps even Acacia had fallen subject.

The boards above me creaked. I was not alone. Perched upon the outside of the barred skylight, that bird, which had ushered me to Acacia, now minded me with its slow-blinking eyes. I lay down on my back, slow, so as not to startle it. By my count, its lids drooped at ten, twelve, then twenty. Finally, its orbs sealed with resound like the big steel door at the fancy bank my father took me to once in Little Rock.

I tried out names for the bird. I liked best Azrael, Anastasia, Methuselah, and Hank.

My bird held something wooden in its talons—a box, eight inches long and two wide, the oak timber rudely engraved with a whittling knife, its large endorsement: "E. Muir." Throbbing hunger, I hoped for nourishment—sweet treats or vulture scavenge, that would also do—and while I entertained these varieties, the talons released, and the wooden box dropped and smote my face flush, and I lay coldcocked in the dirt.

When I woke again and touched my tender face, well-caked in dried blood, the bird was gone. But to my surprise, during my unconscious state, I had accomplished a small errand of Heaven with the contents of the box. It had been filled with rusted gutterspike nails, apparently, for I found I had pushed a dozen of these through each sole of my leather slippers, which I then placed back on my feet. I crooked my leg at the knee to study such a weapon-impractical, viciously spined with the sharpest talons.

Outside my shed, strong winds shifted the ashes; began new blazes when sparks of ember met sprites of green. Through the skylight I watched the sway of the trees. Beyond the branches, dark clouds amassed, and with them, my absinthol soul brewed a strong tea of revenge.

For in this new shed the Son visits often. He holds my chain and speaks of a future meaningless as the abyss. I adopt the fulsome gaze of the betrothed, but silently call in the storm.

And should it finally strike—if lightning signals its search of lamb—if the rivulets of current leap about the earth and through my chain—if a Heavenly sender shows this mercy, then I will lunge for the Son. Sink my tongue into his mouth and undress him — arouse him — grip and stroke him, and all the while pray that lightning strikes once more and renders us to embers.

But the storm demurred. Prudish thunderheads. We fucked in dust through months of drought.

The skin on my face had grown infected. At my pleading, the Son smuggled me a pastel compact from the Nightingale's cosmetics bag so I might see the blight for myself. Corpuscles bloomed from my cheeks, forehead, and neck — small florid teacups, nubbed and wide at the opening. I probed these strange attractions in the small glint of the mirror, gilded lilac, ombre, and cream, emitting a clear pus which heightened their shimmer.

The Son left, but not without another pity present — my little books and pens slid from his shirt as he dashed a kiss to my forehead. To receive them, he made me swear on the bird I would not run again.

In the fourth month of this imprisonment, with my hope but a margin revived, as I drafted and redrafted my arrival to Acacia in these little books, the sky spilled. Genesis floods. Rainwater pooled on the roof of the shed, then ran a channel through a dent in the coping. I lapped the tainted flow. Dustbowl became again a throat.

I passed the time making handshadows on the wall. Of a loathsome golem, a bedeviled rooster who had lost its head, of a vengeful soaring bat.

And I transcribed my dreams and visions:

The pitch of the train's whistle sounds and then bends like a boomerang. I feel encased in a coffin of thick and taxing air and rise to open the window of the Pear House, where Lo! I am now the regent of Heaven.

I peer over the sky, and before my eyes begins a starfall—first one brief flare, then another in the east, followed by a grouping of a half-dozen so close I feel I could pluck them like dandelions. Like a camera's long exposure, the heavens continue their glamour and preserve the glory of each declining body. The sky grows overwhelmed with the bright residue of streaking arcs of light. Against this illumination, all the nesting birds of Acacia's thicket take flight. Crow and grouse, chickenhawk and sparrow, mourning dove and cattle egret congregate heavenward. The birds unite above me in a vast murmurating swoop, cascading across the brightened sky with a ballerina's lilting sway.

And then they return to the Pear House. The birds burst through the window. The chamber fills with their sibilance. The speed of their wings makes a strobe of the starlight.

Behold — their wings transmute into one grand wing.

Then, congeals its arching twin.

The wings span and crook again and shed their runted quills like needles from a dried-out Christmas tree. Forging and fussing into a hulk of chest, a singular wretched neck emerges, wrapped in wild charcoal plume. The neck supports a claret face, its wistful eyes glowering like twin voids. Where there were many hissing beaks, vision clarifies and there remains a single, sharp, yellow shank.

The giant hustles above me, Petra the Wretched, stricken on the floorboards in my pale nightclothes. I raise my thin forearm in barrier. The bird opens its maw and spills raw earth, worms, and sprouting jeweled roots into my wailing mouth. And scream becomes gurgle. And gurgle becomes silence.

For a time, I am fed like this, by my tamer, my torturer. Convalescence, a wonder I begin to understand.

Nourished, my belly rounds. My ribs fill in. The bird's daily return holds hidden knowledge. Its spittle tastes of cinnamon and cardamom and maintains me on the bridge between worlds.

During our last feeding the bird shudders and vomits a river of buck-lead pellets. I sputter but swallow the shotgun's metal, the bird lengthens its neck to kiss its beak to my lips, and its crimson aspect is the mercury hair and stubbled face of the Son . . .

. . . for I was no longer in dream in the Pear House but cradled in his arms in the dirt of the shed in which I remained captive. The Son nuzzled me, having witnessed my tremors. He lamented each abuse. But I was only hungry. I implored him for a handful of dirt. If he'd only release his grip, I'd flatten my jaws to the soil and brux.

The Son visited me on this occasion with a sheaf of papers, a quill pen, and a small container of ink, and when I had calmed, he spread these out in the soil before me like I'd qualified for a big bank loan. His arrival had calmed me, cheered me, until the nature of his errand clarified.

— Should I eat these? I asked. I upset the orderly stack of papers — the deposition of my offenses against the Nightingale and Acacia, her red ink in long, minuscule script across the lined paper. With no cookstove to destroy them, I stuffed a handful into my mouth and chewed until I retched.

— Sign them!

The Son took new tack. He produced a liniment of maple and charred pine from his back pocket, stored in an empty glass jar of Gerber baby food. He massaged the burning ointment across my face and the fresh eruptions covering my legs — dollops of taut bulbous flesh, red as my vulture's aspect; the enduring bodily fruit, perhaps, of the Nightingale's tongue.

— Sign, he appealed, my golden heart of golden hearts. He spoke with such comfort while palpating my angry red shames with the salve — Sign, and then you may eat. Then you may return to the Pear House.

If I could only certify such damnings. Organize each swoop of the Prophetess Mother's longhand and — Sign! — fess my delinquency. So mercurial was the Mother, I'd receive a silver Trans Am as soon as a bite of bread, and I knew no mark of mine would ever earn her graces.

Gentle but unceasing — sign, sign, sign — the Son was a parrot, trained on the single word of its handler. His shirt was open, the collar breached, the buttons undone, the smooth chest I knew so well beneath that cool muslin.

The Son turned for a fresh scoop of the salve. His back to me, I drew my diseased leg. Crooked it at the knee.

When he turned back around — his drooping shirt and chest before me — Sign! slipping off his lips — I struck with the sharpest point of my doctored slippers; a murmuration of nails. I would never succumb. The Son's howls did nothing to hide the sound of the door thundering in behind us. With it came the tyrant in linen.

My panic warped and weft and carried me in its carnival as I stuffed myself against the wall's raw boards. I screamed as her soft flesh enforced a grip about me, and the sounds of the Nightingale's sweet song rose to overcome my outcry like a thick quilt smothers fire. Her hands cradled my face with a boundless patience. She was a mother, afterall, and I calmed in her grip, whimpering like an outmatched cur. Even as the Son stumbled his way out my shed, the Nightingale withheld her anger.

She troubled me this day because of new visions. Perhaps witnessing me over these past months, in trance and documentation in my shed, she desired the balance of my foreknowing.

To carry out whatever good works she had planned for me, I was removed from my shed, bathed, and established in the Pear House in a certain room preserved for ceremony — in the front-facing bedroom of the Nightingale's childhood.

After months alone and abused, I entered the room a tattered duchess. Among the swarm of antiques and relics, drawn curtains and low orange lamps cast a Texas sundown. A kettle, robin's egg blue, softly murmured on an electric camping stove. Laundered nightclothes had been expertly folded and set for me on a highbacked chair. A black-and-white television set on a bar cart soundlessly played *Three's Company*.

In the morning, the Nightingale said, I would share with her whatever revelations the night foretold. She shut the door with the beneficent smile of dominion.

But this was a troubled night. I heard the call of the train, yet the pitch was corrupted, the duration lacking, and I did not trust it. Still, I rose to study the doorknob.

Turn it, Petra. Is it locked? Turn it. Evade the Son in the thicket. Return to your kin of the rails.

But when at last I drew the daring and touched the cold brass knob, something caught in my bowels, and I waited yet longer.

There, at last. Wafting the corridors, tickling the scrubbed crown molding, across the oil paintings of Acacia's founding on either side of the hallway, and through the ancient keyhole of my door, my suspicions were affirmed—the whisperings of the watching Mother.

For the remainder of the night I waited under the bed, with-standing drafts and moans and the intimate scurry of mice and spiders, low-layer creatures of the earth. So entombed, I prayed. For the sake of myself. For any visitation.

Dear Keen Reader,

Reviewing these entries from my precious little books grieves me. Burdened with similar agonies, others have pleaded for an escape hatch, a rope, a gun, a *deus ex machina,* that it be any other scheme of Heaven than the table set before them. Yet still, I fathom the holy sequence. Our woes carve the rut, and through it, Heavenly power courses.

Have you, Reader, discerned the unmatched guile of the Prophetess Mother? The ruses by which she affected the devotion of so many for so long. No, surely not, and I carry the fault. These entries in my little books have largely shown her dominion. Soon, I will detail her beguilements; her peculiar kindnesses, her sweet pollutions. But first I will tell you of the special resistance to poisons both spiritual and earthly that Heaven endowed me with as a child of ten all the way back in the Jesper of my girlhood, for since then my body has been a well-shelved apothecary and no blight can topple me. There is primrose in my fingertips and salted ice in my chipmunk cheeks.

I return the reader to an entry from my little books composed during the duress and torture of my sheds, to a memory transcribed that began at the Caldwell Farm, where even as a little girl I ought to have drawn upon my giftings to suss out Divine mystery before it swept me in its tides.

BOOK V

And there I went, ten years old, long after bedtime, creeping down the stairs of the Caldwell farmhouse in a ragged lace nightgown for a swallow of cold milk. Snatches of sound — low, rumbly, and familiar — gave me pause. It was my parents, fervently in prayer:

— Tent . . . Fire . . . Our Daughter . . . Heaven . . . Holiday . . . .

Their words lit me with jubilee. I gave up on the drink and snuck back upstairs to stuff my backpack with the necessary provisions for this upcoming camping trip: a flashlight, a hardbound copy of *Alice in Wonderland* with black and white illustrations, extra jeans, a white blouse, and a pleated holiday dress for no other reasons than to be prepared. I brought along my whittling project too: a small bird carved from a block of live oak, along with the rusty Old Timer tri-blade my father had managed when he was a boy. Wrestling the supplies into my pack, I startled when my mother announced herself.

Behold, my mother — she leans against the doorframe, the curve of her hip like the round of a scythe, her belly heavy, for soon she would give birth to my sister. She must have watched me packing for long moments, buttressing herself with my joy. But then she

settled down on her knees to deliver me the wasp-sting news.
My disappointment did then flow, ferocious as a burst hydrant.

Boons such as a camping trip were rare jewels at the Caldwell
Farm, she knew this and said as much. But this trip was not
for me. I would not be coming. This was their errand, her and
Father's. And a special charge at that, bespoke by Heaven.
Embracing me with her finely hewn arms, which I had once
seen piledrive a frenzied sow like the wrestlers did on Saturday
night television, she confided of their gorgeous errand. She and
Father would venture off into the woods to camp, to a special
place. There, they would deliver this new boon to our family and
christen my sister under the starlight and the trees.

A week thereafter, Mother subdued her bouncy curls under her
red handkerchief and knelt in the soggy dewgrass to freshen the
pucker of my sleeves. She drew back for her inspection, then
thumbed my nose and called it good. Father, meanwhile, gave
no glance my way, but saw to the truck, holding his sacred black
book under his arm while running the dipstick along a thin piece
of wadded tissue, offering choice language toward the balding
tires. I was remaindered alone in our farmhouse with a single
command:

—You will not leave these grounds.

And leave the farm I did not wish to do, for contagion ravaged our town and the surrounding region. For weeks, inhabitants, nearby farmers, and passers-through pausing for a homestead meal had contracted some gruesome affliction. At the origin they grew limp in their limbs. Then came an onset of bubbleguts followed by high fever and ramblings. Sufferers clutched themselves about the stomach, bowling over as excrement and retch erupted from both ends. Rendered to sick camps in decrepit barns on the outskirts of Jesper, their skin assumed a strange yellow crust like curdled milk on the gallon's lip. There were casualties, marked near the treeline on a small hill with hastily fashioned wooden crosses. The papers, which Father read aloud to us at breakfast, said bad meat from a Texas slaughterhouse. But the Spirit in Father said, doomsday, doomsday, doomsday.

I watched my parents depart on their righteous commission, clunking away up Long Bow Avenue, then turning left to drive all day toward their secret spot off in the big thicket that Mother had described. And all the while, I imagined them as Mother had intimated: pinned together in a holy union on a newly stitched quilt atop the nettles and pinecones, weathering what would surely be her difficult labor, though afterwards, holding my sister in her swaddling clothes, luxuriating with jugged water, mustard dogs, and bison jerky around the steady embers of a blessed campfire.

Our homestead served me fine in these lone hours. The first day, I gave into laziness and naps and television and jump-rope. But by the morning next, I began to fear my lassitude would be discovered and took up my labor as the dutiful daughter. I fixed a breakfast of thin pork cutlets and drank the dregs of stale coffee from Father's speckled thermos. Then I tended the soiled cast iron with coarse salt and steel wool, mopped the begrimed linoleum back to its true shade, and stacked the china near the icebox. Then, I returned the floral sheets and faded quilts from the clothesline to the linen closet.

Next to the closet loomed my parents' bedroom. Limp from my labors, I stepped across the threshold. I knew well the room's habits and placements. Knew the crinkling paisley wallpaper, sun-bleached from the drawn curtains, and Mother's jewelry dish—an old porcelain ashtray sprinkled with small copper rings and titanium studs that sat on the battered, antique armoire— and where Father's good Laredo boots would be, had he been home. Knew the dresser topped with the Pendleton blanket and the empty aquamarine vase that hadn't seen a fresh flower in my memory. I ran my hand along the frame of their tarnished brass bed and hot and cold tingles rippled through me like a dram of whiskey. I was forbidden to linger, surely, I was. But throughout the spell of my temptation, I knew this shiny lure and knew it well: bedding could be so easily straightened.

And so, I set aside the soup pot catching a roof leak, and leapt into their bed, and cast off the throw pillows to dishevel morning discipline. I burrowed underneath Mother's Arkansas state motto quilt, probing the delicacy of her needlework with my fingertips. And then I doubled Father's pillow under my head and occupied myself with the reason for this soup pot: directly over their bed—descending from the ceiling and swole with rainwater—was a giant plaster breast.

The bosom was a new arrival to my parents' room. Occasioned by spates of summer hail, a fissure had developed in the roof. As the storms flowed through the tributaries of the busted shingles and into the innards of the rafters, angling toward the household crux, a bubble of thinning plaster, a whale's eye, drip-by-drip stretched and filled. Grandeur shaped by storms, the breast was at first the yellow-white of the ceiling, but shaded to a grey ombre as the plaster bloated, ending in a slate-colored nipple that discharged a steady drip.

Giving in again to leisure, I stood up on the bed and leaned my warm cheek against its cool spongy bubble. I placed my palms to its side and nursed it; a lukewarm water, sweet as pop. I thought hard for a time if I had suckled my own mother. I could not recall one. I ducked back under the comforter and gave myself to fancy:

To the red spray from a severed chicken gullet; to cotton candy clouds at sunset, incinerating like turbid newspaper in a wood-stove. I thought about running with three legs instead of two, with four, with six, with sixty. I thought about my mother, and my sister, who was maybe just now rending her way into the world with Heaven's expedience.

And I see my mother's legs part open and a rosebud skull, slick with birth sap, pushing forward and blooming into a babe — and I see my mother's legs give way to reveal a dark cave from which a basilisk rears, scorching my father with an exhalation of hell-fire — and I see this cave again, and a slim, tiny figure greets me: a naked sister, crawling forward.

The following morning, I rose unrested and straightened out the damp bedding, regretful I had not returned the pot to its station before I fell asleep.

To soothe my gurgling hunger, I sopped canned beans with a piece of molding Texas toast. The winds kicked up. As I ate, I wondered after my parents. I hoped they might arrive by evening latest. But perhaps their errand had not taken. Perhaps they were rekindling the flames and resuming the delivery among the nettles. Father had fortitude; Mother, spunk aplenty.

I thought these things while slowly clearing the dishes and, so enraptured I was, I did not spy the man until he was but two dozen feet from our porch. He went without pants or under-clothes, though he wore a soiled dress shirt that curtained his pecker. He seemed to walk a maze of his own dizzying design, toppling now and again like a spent wooden top to turn out his guts into the bushes. A few more steps and there followed his bowels among Mother's hot pink portulacas.

The man reached the porch before he spied me in the window. His skin was ravaged with swollen, open sores. His eyes were milky things, dead of twinkle. His droughted lips pulsed like a wartime wiretap.

The wretched angel raised his palms so I might see his good intent. But for all my moxie, I cast my lot with the coward's and quit the house from the back door. I kept my small red bike back there. When I pedaled around the house, I witnessed the man set upon our handsome four-paned window with the wooden stool on which Father took his pipe. He let himself in through the shards, through Mother's prim lace curtains.

As for me, I pedaled toward Jesper two miles hence. Town of the blinking four-way stop, where Saturday is grass-mowing day, and Johnny Cash is God.

Under usual circumstances, July 4th would show Jesper's Main Street emblazoned with flag bunting, strung white lights canopying the street, sparklers blistering, and the small town out for play. But the outbreak had rendered the place a sorry sight for independence.

At the north end of town, framed by a gas station and an empty fruit stand, a diminished parade of celebrants had yet gathered in the street. The Mayor served as the Captain of Ceremonies. Mounted on a speckled mare, he raised a dented trumpet to his lips and blew a squealing bleat. The marching band behind him struck up a martial tune, but the recent sickness showed its hand in their diminished ranks: a pockmarked snare player beat along with a bass drummer, and that was that for rhythm. A lone junior tuba and gangly twin flautists served for the brass. To compensate their play, the Mayor tipped his chin skyward and blew sour notes as he deemed complementary. I leaned low atop my handlebars as they commenced the parade, shamed to account, I remained in my nightgown.

After the band came a farmer herding a rust-colored sow with a leather pig whip. Then a new John Deere Iron Horse that had never seen a day in the field, followed by a dice-throw of Shriners in their little, hand-built cars. And finally, a few children on roller skates, who threw out ample handfuls of golden butterscotch from brown paper sacks. They could spare it, for as far as I could see, we onlookers were a scant dozen.

Up the road, a Shriner split off from the group and parked his car in front of Jesper's tavern. I found myself with a measure of time to spare, and so I followed him, resting my bike against the railing of the stairs, hoping there might be snacks inside to settle my stomach until Father returned to send the intruder on to his eternal reward.

At the threshold, I surveyed a bustling crowd communing inside the tavern. Under the yellow glow of electric sconces and beer neon signs, a dozen men in coveralls sat at the long bar, sucking down skunky green lagers. Rough folks at a card table accosted a barmaid in blue plaid, who made no hurry in supplying them a tray of squat bourbon tumblers. The wooden floor before me was well scuffed, an indication the room occasioned dancing, or maybe fights between drunks settling their scores. In the corner, a jukebox turned over the patchman, Dick Curless's, "A Tombstone Every Mile."

No sooner had I stepped inside than a gaunt woman with possum eyes shoved me backward, directly under the gold illumination of an Olympia beer sign. She peered me over like a brooding biddy, running judgment across my arms, neck, and face. Satisfying herself I was free of the blight, she leaned back into the shadows and resumed conversing with her man.

The barmaid saw it all. From behind her barricade at the rear of the room she waved me over. I crossed the dancefloor and sat where she indicated, in the corner stool beneath an array of taxidermied birds mounted on the wall. She disappeared for a moment beneath the bar and returned with a lunch carton of milk. She had, in certain light, the beatific visage of a saint; in others, as she slung drinks and made change, the menacing jowls of a bulldog.

A calmness settled over me as the occasion for the tavern's gathering clarified. The room emptied to either side, leaving a wide space in the center of the dancefloor. From the swinging saloon doors leading to the street, a lanky man with dark, slicked-back thinning hair entered the bar. He wore a fine salmon tuxedo and a large cloth bowtie. Nerves flashed across his face like television static. Someone passed him a shot glass and he drained it in a go. The barmaid unplugged the jukebox and took up a small guitar, which she tuned with expedience. Shushing the crowd with a growl, she began picking out a charming wedding march.

I stood weakly on my stool for a better look, my head among the ruffled breast feathers of a stuffed pheasant. From the kitchen, the bride came slow. She was veiled and carried a bouquet and wore a white gown of festooned lacework with a dramatic sequined train that bunched and shuffled behind her like a pageant of intoxicated swans. She joined the bridegroom in the center of the room. He took her gloved hands as though they were made of eggshells, and they moved together toward the jukebox to face the barmaid.

As the bride turned, for the first time I viewed her back. From her bottom to the floor, where the dress flowed into the ground, long streaks of wet brown polluted the train.

Jesper's kinfolk kept a wide berth from the twain — these lovers, married soon buried — crowding themselves further into the hot corners of the room like mice seeking shadow. It was a brief ceremony, during which I eyed trays of champagne for the toasts, poured in advance into Pan Am Airways plastic teacups. Crisp, tangy, better than mother's milk, the liquid steadied me. I helped myself to another.

When the bridegroom had removed her veil, and when her kiss was gently met, and when the pronouncements were thereafter made, the bride gave of her strength and heaved her bouquet. It sailed beneath the dim yellow lights in wide twirls, end-over-end, the crinkled ribbons like big city fireworks, and the guests scattered as if receiving a grenade. They were scrubby country flowers, picked from the levee's brittle soil. And when they met my outstretched hands, it was with a burst of twig, leaf, and petal; it was disintegration in my palms, for the entire nosegay was dead.

The barmaid's nod suggested I go. I took her hint and faltered out onto Main Street. It was early evening, Jesper was deserted, and I was stumbling drunk.

My timing was magnificent, for entering the road I spied my parents slowly driving toward me. My father sat grim behind the wheel of the truck; my mother likewise wore her worry.

As I soon came to know, an hour past, upon returning to the farmhouse, Father had discovered the broken window. He proceeded with his rifle, searching the interior of the house until he found the intruder, sprawled upon their soiled bed, expired. The distended breast above the man had finally burst and the split panels of wet plaster hung from the roof like skinned cattle. The deluge had soaked the dead man through.

We could not yet return to the farmhouse, Father informed me, as we struggled back into the truck. Not in its afflicted state. And so we sheltered in Jesper's cheapest motel instead. Father took his shower while Mother and I sat together with our backs against the headboard, the crook of her arm a cool, welcome haven.

As I returned from the hazy carousel of my stolen drinks, I became aware of Mother's belly, still heavy beneath the worn cotton of her dress. We watched *My Living Doll* on the small box TV, which set Mother with distant, red-rimmed eyes and a forlorn smile, and I could not resist loving her and studying her with the sneak of my eye as her trembling hands tenderly stroked the grand heap of Heaven's miracle yet beneath her dress. When she noticed my attentions, for she was of the perceptive kind who could spot the very first mill bug in a barrel of flour, she invited me to lay my ear against her belly and speak a tender word. And so I did, calling my sister blessed, mischievous, a believer in fairies, a volunteer, a kindred, and I did then feel the drip of Mother's warm tears fall against the back of my neck.

When Father returned from the bathroom, Mother took her turn. Father changed the channel to the ball game and raised the volume so loud we could not talk. But I found no diversion in the game. My stomach had begun to heave. I lay back on the crisp, rose-print comforter. And when my guts felt they would give at any moment, I quit Father and burst into the bathroom to relieve myself.

Inside stood Mother, her back to me. She was naked and wore a strange contraption about her body. Thick leather straps, like those used to harness oxen, were cinched around her shoulders.

They crossed her back in an X, and then wrapped around her waist. The straps were secured with burnished brass buckles. As she turned to me, worn and weary, I perceived that the straps doubled over the front of her body, where they held up a heavy leather apron that stretched from her hips to just beneath her breasts. Within the apron, a large smooth river stone sat firmly cradled against her stomach, which was swollen still, but clearly no longer carrying a child.

Mother beckoned me in with great concern. With one hand, she guided me to the toilet, where I expelled the fruits of Jesper's poison. And with the other, she stroked Heaven's miracle — my sister, the stone.

Dear Searching Reader,

If my body is an apothecary, in Jesper began my immunity against a dark rainbow of toxicants.

Of the entries I share with you from my little books, let them now begin to bloom different shades of the Prophetess Mother Nightingale's dominion. Let them show sunbeam and tea, boons and charming bonds, so that the fullness of her artifice be known. Here are entries of my early years in Acacia, just as I was growing into my full power and yet beset with the Nightingale's tortures. I return the reader to my captivity in the Pear House, after I had harmed the Son with my violent slippers, and most significant of all, to the birth of Fleur's promised Boy, a portented sovereign of our sacred hamlet whose consequence and heritage you will appreciate in full as my account unfolds.

BOOK VI

THE CHILDHOOD BEDROOM
of the NIGHTINGALE
& HER PORTRAITS
& A BODILY EXAMINATION
and its ENSUING PROPHECY
& RAGE
& THE STAGING of a PLAY
& TO JUDGE the MOTHER,
if YET in VISION
& THE BIRD APPEARS at LAST
& A THICKET TEMPEST
& THE BIRTH of the PROMISED BOY

This is the room of the Nightingale's girlhood. Herein, I was kept as the Mother visited me to ask after my dreams and command me to comment upon hers. Grand and decayed, the den was a forgotten storehouse for dusty relics, for glass bottles and blue porcelain bowls, for small gilded emblems and cedar cigar boxes. Velvet fainting couches with thick macrame trim rested about the large space, thoroughly dusted with cinder. The walls defleshed their filigree-bouqueted paper, even to the expansive ceilings, where a luminous crystal chandelier reigned from the center of the room like an ancient queen. A diminutive carved walnut bed sat against the back wall, threatened by the overwhelm of mementos. And the paintings. As the Christ child is portrayed in a wooden manger, overlooked by prosperous mystics, a glowing mother, and a collection of mules, fowl, and horned goats, so too in this room were significant moments of the Nightingale's mythos told in portrait.

I drifted among them. In one she appeared in a bassinet with a silver bonnet, silver coverlet, and a silver binkie, eyes smoldering amidst wisps of blonde curls; in another, pictured at twelve, she was lithe and mercenary, and she carried a longbow drawn with a silver arrow. The artist had painted her with wings, and she hovered above a stampede of foxes, preparing to spear the skulk's champion. In another painting the Nightingale wept over a grave, planted in a curious garden growing wildly from a bedframe, as silver smoke billowed about her like a collective of watchful shades.

From the windows of the bedroom I surveilled Acacia's grounds. The men with the rakes faithfully tilled their garden. The women ferried their candles in jars to the chapel. The children played freeze tag. And for a time, there was the bird—a dark blur and constant distraction—darting in and out of the corners of my vision like a brazen house mouse.

On the day before the Nightingale's promised Boy was born to Fleur, our young sorceress of the kitchen, the Mother Salome called all Acacia to the table in the Pear House. I too was permitted to attend—a special leave from my lockup in the room upstairs. To the Acacians' surprise, Fleur lay waiting atop the long banqueting table, her white dress pulled up and over her bare, bulging stomach.

As Fleur leaned up on her elbows, the Nightingale dipped her fingers in oil and slid them around the young woman's belly, palpating this orb, probing at the little bird trapped inside. From the womb, the child did thrust back.

The Nightingale howled, her face contorting as if hot coals had been pressed into her underarms. She did then climb upon the table so all could view her and revealed to us her palms. The soft flesh was angry, red and blotchy as crushed raspberries. And then the Nightingale threw back her head and prophesied, of which I summarize:

Fleur would carry a child of the sword into the bastion of plenty we called Acacia. Scythe wheels would thresh, and night obtain. The Commotions were Heaven's blotting, inbound now from the eternities of Heaven, not yet here, though we would see their advent. And this child our Fleur carried, this Boy, he would be our champion. Our precious opal and our store of munitions. Our city on a hill when the earth's last day of phantom paramountcy arrived.

Before my very eyes Acacia's devotion expanded. We held each other, poured out our gratitude to Fleur. First, we had a Nightingale. Now, Fleur would carry Acacia its deliverer in the Commotions, the horrendous rending doomsday we so earnestly prayed would pass us by.

Returned to the privacy of my prison room after this impromptu consecration, I raged. I raged at my sorry compatriots, neglectful of my elegant prophecies, harvested out of me by the Mother to earn my bread—I raged at the Mother herself for her naming of another even while she had found such a capable surrogate in me—and I raged at Heaven, for its marathon of torments, each mile more excruciating than the last. For months imprisoned in that room during the latter part of Fleur's pregnancy, I had sought my bird and raged.

Rage without recourse, though I had a taste of the judgment seat once before in a play with my middle-school classmates. There hung in the air, as we commenced our first rehearsal, a trinity of scent & affect—citrus, pungent, and nauseating—for these were the stenches seeping off the pendant my Jesper classmate and longstanding crush, John Mosley, placed around my neck to costume me, behind the secondhand shop on Main, in the latter half of eighth-grade.

The pendant was a fancy statement piece to match my crown, which John Mosley had shaped from the gossamer-laden rosebush clinging to the outer wall of his mother's beauty parlor. But all we could find for the pendant was an air freshener from the gas station, shaped like Texas. John Mosley tied it around my neck, so it rested against my judge's robe, on the welcome, recent swell of my chest, on the thin fabric, which was white. Which was culled from my mother's fitted sheets, and these bleached-well, and with a hole cut in the center for my head. I would pay this due later, for I was growing into my own, and while the threat of my father's wrath still warmed, it no longer screamed the kettle.

John Mosley set the crown on my head while a dozen of our class-mates solemnly knelt before me. I took my throne: the dented hood of a rusted-out truck, stripped of its tires, the interiors bleached by sunbeam, the whole of the hulk resting on cinder blocks.

This may have been our first rehearsal, but I took my role with urgency. John Mosley ushered the accused before me. I prepared to hear the case, and meet this casting choice for the first time. John Mosley removed the black trash bag from the accused's head. A ripple of whispers shot through our schoolmates, who had assumed the staggered poses of a bloodthirsty crowd— kneeling, raised on one knee—crouching over with hands on the thighs—standing straight with arms akimbo—palms spread over gasping lips—fingers raking sandy blonde hair. And as for me, preparing to levy judgment and fulfill my given role, my breath stopped like a horse had kicked me in the heart, for John Mosley had delivered me my bane—our classmate, and my great dread, Carolynn Peters.

Lord, did I want to punish her—for the way she'd mocked my mother, bloating her cheeks and stuffing her sweatshirt with a volleyball, which slipped out and rolled into the tall grass; for calling me "Miss Mashed Potatoes" in a year when I grew plump around the middle; for convincing the boys the affliction I carried in my quivering lip was caused by some contagious illness; for spying me in the tree as the frothing jaws of a rabid Blue Heeler leapt for my feet—with her clean-jaw smile and a barbarous wave, Carolyn pedaled off and left me to wait some three hours until Father found me and shot the dog dead from the cab of his truck.

Lord, had I imagined enacting my fancy with Carolynn Peters; for many long, leisure hours. There was not a torture device I hadn't strapped her into—stretching—quartering—piercing—scalding. I had watched her step onto landmines in a field of wheat, and her face when the implant registered her pressure; watched her flee down a thin hall where awaited a winged daemon; watched her stomach gored out by a bull. I wanted to tie her down and kiss her lips and run my tongue all over her perfect face. Pluck out her eyes, and if blue had a taste, I'd mulch it. But what I wanted, truly, more than anything, was to shatter her porcine soul.

Carolynn was sweet on John Mosley, and I on John, and John on my mother. We were a venomous triad. The saccharine Texas pendant made me a new kind of nauseous. On Carolynn Peters' bare white shoulder, a *fleur-de-lis* had been crudely emblazoned with a marker, for our teacher, Mr. Shook, had assigned us Dumas and left us to our own devices for its adaptation. I raised my gavel—a twirl girl baton from the thrift store—and fell deeply into trance.

A soul such as Carolynn Peters' was censurable in all possible worlds—of rape—robbery—usury—assault—homicide— larceny—kidnapping—conspiracy—false pretenses—arson —forgery—breach of the peace—blasphemy—espionage— mayhem—petty treason—running a disorderly house—and failure to appear. I lowered my baton with a tsar's final judgment and condemned the void of Carolynn Peters.

John Mosley hauled her up. Carolynn sobbed for mercy; his, mine. But John seemed to have soared in murderous grandeur, like they'd never necked. He hauled her to the edge of the secondhand shop, where the chain link fence stopped, where she laid her chin against a stump framed by ocean waves cutout from cardboard and painted blue with cheap Crayola watercolors. Her final vista—our stagecraft rendering of the cliffside of coastal France.

John Mosley produced a garden rake. Left in the sun, the wide plastic had warped into strange twisting tines. John looked over the sea. How had Heaven selected him the executioner? Grief would haunt this lifetime; traumas such as this would bleed into the next. He raised his rake. He severed her head.

All at once, Carolynn ducked her head inside the loose collar of her nightgown. A pimpled gourd dropped to the ground and rolled unnaturally as the deft arms of a stagehand hidden behind the beheading stump purged a spool of tangled red yarn. Splayed in the loose dirt, her corpse did then convulse. John Mosley fled into the woods. I reached out to him, calling him to come to me and be comforted, as my crown toppled off my head.

And then one evening in my prison of the Pear House, standing afore the locked window sash, I felt a strange stillness creep over me, and my lip quiver yet again, and I felt the judgment seat affect its rest beneath me. And a vision did then come forth like an old black-and-white feature, like the kind the Mother loved to screen on a sheet in the Pear House on a whirling projector . . .

. . . and I see myself once again upon the seat, exalted on a dais, surrounded by my lessers, and wearing a black robe and a powdered wig and curlers. A bang of the gavel and the Prophetess Mother Salome Nightingale bows her head. Her stench is revolting, like scorched Vaseline. Small and frail and in rags, she crawls before me with the muculent stalling of a garden snail.

— Salome Nightingale!

[I deliver it with the sonorous let-my-people-go from Moses.]

. . . For treason against Heaven, how do you plead?

— I am innocent. Who are you to judge me?

— Will you call a witness?

—I will.

[I am humored.]

—Whom would you call?

—I will call Petra.

[Gasps sweep the Acacians in the courtroom.]

[I am amused.]

—You will call me?

—I will.

—On what account?

—The truth of my testimony, and the power of arcana
   vested in me, the Mother.

                    [Rocking back in my chair, scoffing.]
—Yours is an effort of biding time.

—You are the witness I call, though you now carry the
    gavel.

                    [All attendees nod and murmur.]

    . . . Petra . . .
                            [So quietly under her pile of rags
                            she may as well be buried . . .]
. . . might you look long upon me and find a measure
    of revelation? For if you won't, then I will look
    at *you*. I will look . . .
                            [she says it again, and I stand
                            as she approaches me . . .]
. . . I will look at length; I look into your face, a
    mold lacking eyebrows and eyes and full lips,
    sallowed, smithereened; I am looking. I am
    delving through your leper's mouth and past
    your sickly throat, and still, I burrow on, and I
    uncover what? Is it this?

[her voice grows louder . . .]
. . . your soul-spine, withered like a kitchen pipe
    beset with lime? Is this what you want me to
    find? This is nothing. Through and through,
    nothing. I extract from your recesses, and
    return to my voice, and you, standing before
    your chair holding that silly gavel. But wait,
    what's this?

*[here, she appears to receive her
own vision and then stares upon
me with incendiary eyes . . .]*

. . . from your craven head, shoots a kettle of
    vultures, chased from the comfort of their
    trees. Somewhere in their expanse, in their
    plummet, two, selected by Heaven, labor
    in a cave, and from its opening a stone rolls
    forth covered in white mold and yellow pus,
    wobbling its way to sink into the oblivion of a
    crick. A child will find it one day, this stone.

*[the room silent as a stuffy
museum, her voice, a hair
above a whisper.]*

[I am enraged.]

— What is this vision, Salome? The beginning of the
    Commotions? Heaven's terror flails in the wind
    like a dimestore kite. Is this the Boy you've
    consecrated? Who is the Boy to you, Salome?
    Who but diversion; who but extension? The
    bloody red you smeared across our foreheads
    after fondling Fleur's stomach? I saw it, I tasted
    it—the dark juice of Buffalo currants, applied by
    sleight of hand. And the Boy, fess it, Salome. Fess
    it and I will let you see him—he was nothing but
    a dowry to secure the saints for a while longer;
    nothing but a push-up bra to woo a bridegroom.

[The Mother holds steady earth . . .
            for a moment . . .
                before buckling.]

— All is forgiven, Petra. But grind your teeth; seethe
    and rage me if you must. Make believe you
    haven't foretold all this in your dreams. Turn
    to the last page of your precious little books.
    Heaven has ordained your ending.

[Such gaul the Prophetess has,
even in my visions!]
— You may not unwrite my sheds, you may not find
absolution with the language of mirage. I will not
permiss it!

. . . but mirage, that is all these visions are. Even my bird is
mirage. A *Fata Morgana*. An unreliable miracle. The Mother's
trial concluded, I have nearly convinced myself this is true—
that nothing and no one will save me—when outside my prison
window, my locked cell at the Pear House, the bird shows itself
at last.

Pillows of clouds spread to either side behind its wings, and it
hovers before me, still and fixed like the diamond totem in a
grand dame's necklace. Its claret face is rich as cherry juice. I
place my palms against the glass and crave it diagnose my soul,
that it pick me clean of aberrant lumps. The bird's affection
for me is patient; absurd. Damn the glass keeping me. Damn
the glass!

I step upon the cherry arm of a divan and extend my arms. Not flapping, but pricking, probing, for a current. The lace curtains I'd wound around me shed like molting skin. The desiring eyes of Acacia's chorus look upon my nakedness from the garden below. The Nightingale joins them. I can pick out their song.

— Congregation, witness rapture.

> *[From the rail of the couch, I leap.*
> *Harnessing the spring of the*
> *cushion to propel me forward, the*
> *weight of my frame carries me*
> *through the old glass.]*

. . . I will wing the heavens. Join my bird and quit
    this place and ascend to the mysteries in the
    clouds so often teased . . .

. . . but to the ground I plunged.

Soft earth cushioned the full shock from my body, facedown in the garden's fresh till. Bugs prodded me with their tiny pads. Memory carried me back to the Caldwell Farm, to my father in a rare moment of joy, drunk and dancing randily with my mother to the Allman Brothers, and how when he caught sight of me—standing in the doorframe of the kitchen in my little yellow dress imitating the thrust of his pelvis—he fell to the floor and guffawed till he cried.

Like this coarse gagman, my breath finally returned too, in heaves and tears, with bitter laughter, for my bird had called in vision, and when I had followed in body, it had forsaken me.

The Nightingale approached; a small-footed stalk. She pressed the iron of her rake to the side of my neck. A flick of her wrist, a right turn, and the heavy teeth of the rake would bleed me out.

Perhaps my bird was fearful, for asudden, the sky shaded through with a nauseous green hue and a chorus of wind whipped across the clearing, turning Acacia's nearby treeline berserk. Though none of the saints could see the tempest coming, none mistook the magnitude of its sound—like a fury of warhorses—the death knell of a wooden rollercoaster—lightning in a glass room. Funnel clouds touched down in the thicket like Heaven's marionettes and churned toward the Pear House.

A distinct cry, long and inflamed, rose from one of the second-floor open windows. It was a young woman's voice; I knew it as Fleur's. In her button of childbirth, another cry soon followed; this one, from her newborn child. Finally, a third voice—a thicket whisper discernible even in the pandemonium—*puer natus est nobis, puer natus est nobis, puer natus est nobis*—announced that a child had been born.

I raised my head and rested my cheek on the ruptured soil only to witness holy mess: Acacia was in frenzy as the saints fled the storm. Rakes went abandoned in the garden. Long skirts were pulled around the women's knees, their candles and jars cast aside, to run. Children were hauled-up, screaming, by their waist bands. A glimpse into the ataxia when Heaven would finally deliver the Commotions.

All sought shelter but the Nightingale. She alone remained, poised above me. The wind had unbound her long, deep red hair and it whorled straight into the sky like a flaming dunce cap. The layers of her garments—her skirts and shawls—flared about her body like the thrumming brushes in a drive-thru carwash. Her bird eyes had dilated to black spheres. And still, her rake rested firmly against my neck. The Mother heard the cries from the Pear House too, and I watched as her competing appetites diverged. Punish Petra the Wretched in the barrows? Or greet this newborn child?

Greatness revels in crisis, sees the hidden pathwork in the puzzle, rolls up its sleeves and tends the garden. In a twirling of muslin, the Nightingale left me to the winds and skipped toward the Pear House. She had promised this child to Acacia. In him rested hope and future. She would meet her Boy.

Replacing the Mother's discipline, Heaven tendered me the full measure of its passion as brambles and thorns and gasoline and splintered planks and the fear of the small creatures of the thicket swept up as the cat-o'-nine-tails and whipped across my body. How would I be found?

Nude, lacerated, seizured.

In the bedlam that strange stillness settled again about my body; a thrumming attunement to the storm. It was as though a thousand wings had uniformly fluttered, cutting the air in identical cadence. Or like the sonorous, single, warm-up note the Houston symphony struck before playing Brahm's No. 1 on a Jesper High fieldtrip when I was a freshman. The entirety of the storm's natural lawlessness folded in on itself and reached a perfect swelling pitch, and I was overtaken in its ecstasy.

But my eyesight—this belongs to Heaven. Though my body lay ravaged in the garden, I would behold what it wished, and at its whim.

. . . and lissomly, Heaven takes control of my perception and snakes it over the grounds and through the front door of the Pear House, over apoplectic saints amassed in the doorframes and closets and inner corners, and up the stairs, and down the long hall, before stopping at the door of a certain room. Then it carries my sight across the threshold, for Heaven wishes me to behold this wonder:

Lit by storm light alone, in the center of the room stands an ornate bassinet, hand-carved and elegantly dusted with rose gold, all enclosed with humble moth-devoured draping. A swath of cream-lattice swaddling cloth nuzzles the precious consignment inside:

Heaven carries my sight closer. I peer over the cradle's lip at what lies within:

—Beautiful meat of the Nightingale's desire, Fleur's
    body, and Heaven's will—You are but a babe!
                    [Carry me close, Heaven; perch my
                         spirit over him, this sweet child,
                               pink and rubbery.]
. . . Boy, ruffle in my soft underbelly. When you are
    beneath me, it is to expend my best parts, that
    you may nourish on my wretch. Having broken
    from Fleur's body—Squall! so that the pillars of
    the earth dissolve—so that I know you breathe.

Mother Salome, you brokered your dominion; split it, like wedge
and maul through log. What did you heave from the place of your
presentiment that even I revered his birthing? The portentous
image remains with me, Salome—the red on your hands, passing
palm-to-forehead as you transferred us the Boy's blessing. You
hacked through each of our resistances, piercing our webby neb-
ulas like an adventurer does the foliage, until you reached the

locus amoenus—that deep place, where souls renew and beliefs are shaped—and there you planted the hooks of his legacy.

He could have been born a simple, crying, shitting baby. But when you were done with Acacia that day, on the table with Fleur before you—when you had dissected the saints so adeptly, and each of us bore a red stripe across our brow, blood or berry juice or Heaven's holy oil—he was a rearing shadow on a lantern-lit wall.

He was a breathing promise in a circle of saints who would violently defend his suzerainty.

Dear Renewing Reader,

Desperation requires new modes of worship. A new bride. Fresh wonders. The Mother sensed Heaven's wavering pleasure with her. Though she fought it to the last, The Nightingale knew somewhere in her broken soul that mine was a necessary role.

And I had played many necessary roles in the world I'd left behind.

I return the reader to the Caldwell farm in Arkansas, to me as a girl of ten, and to my mother, six months after the burial of my stone sister, as she knelt beside her small plot in her garden. Behold my mother, still dressed in mourning clothes, still veiled, weeping over the headstone of a stone. What followed was a year of danger.

On one chilly January day, months after the Jesper plague parade, I played in the backyard with a leather quiver and a small wooden bow I had found in the woods. My father had taken ill with Epstein-Barr that late-November and his frailty compelled him to the overstuffed chair in the living room. He had a view of the backyard there, and when my mother had concluded her daily memorial, she remained me to his obligation during one of his few waking spells, thereby excusing herself to bathe upstairs.

Thusly, my father glared at me, his undesired charge, while outside, I braided a lucky feather—a white-tipped roadrunner quill—into my hair and chased imaginary cowboys and shot them dead. I rubbed thick red loam across my cheeks in double stripes. I climbed the mountaintop of my rusted yellow swingset and perched atop the monkey bars to scout for retaliatory bandits. And these my fancy spied, for crossing the backyard on horseback, five brutal Cowboy Apostles rode hard, armed and aiming for my life.

As I removed my quiver and prepared to jump to the ground and return my deadly bowfire, I mis-stepped about the cold, metal monkey bars and slipped between them. But the thick leather strap of my quiver had doubled over the bars and looped in on itself. As I fell forward, my neck slipped into the makeshift noose, my feet dangling inches above the ground.

I fought my hanging, kicking something fierceful, but the ligature tightened, and my vision wavered into bright blurs and soaring spectacles. Before I lost consciousness, I spied my father through the paneled square glass of the back door. And he saw me. Enervated by sickness, he yet fought himself to his feet. He tottered there for a moment, bent at the waist like an old man, before his body lost its grit and he slipped back into the enveloping cushions of his old, beat-up La-Z-Boy. I saw him struggle up again.

He had not managed the yard in months. He received as his penance thirty-two thorns in his bare left foot and twenty-seven in his right before he released me, insensible and blue-skinned, from the backyard gallows of my swingset.

A few months later, as Father permitted me to press the red igniter button on our gas barbecue grill, a faulty regulator and full propane tank combined to release an explosive fireball from the grate. At my eye-level, the flames issued forth and parted around me like Moses' Red Sea, such that while I went untouched, the flare singed the hair off Father's hands and arms, and, as he lunged forward to remove me, devoured even his mustache, eyelashes, and eyebrows.

Later that summer, when I assisted Father in repairing the shingles on the roof, I took a step backwards and fell through the glass skylight and into the living room, where I landed flat on my back on the couch, as if I'd only plopped myself down to binge cartoons on a lazy Saturday morning.

Then in August, on a shopping trip in Jesper for essentials, Mother damned propriety and let me ride in the shopping cart despite that I was ten years old, for just that week I'd learned from my crush, John Mosley, of Richard Petty's boycott of NASCAR and the deadly swerve of his ferocious Hemi Barracuda. This indulgence Mother was thankful to have allowed, for as she steered me about grimly in her long, black mourning dress, a sinister man followed us about the grocery. Mother extended her errand, rerouting to aisles we had already visited, as if we needed another jar of mayonnaise or a second mop, only to observe the man persistently following our circuitous path. Finally checking out, Mother was relieved to find the man had taken leave. She wheeled us to the truck and began unloading the groceries, tucking them behind the passenger seat, and when turning around for the final bag, caught the man gripping me under the arms and yanking me from the cart. Before she had even chance to cry out, the man's visage at once contorted to mysterium, as though fascinated by some numinous vision of the Divine before him, and he stumbled to the ground and scuttled off on his bottom and palms like a terrified crab before disappearing into a line of cars. When mother drove the truck around to give him her demon words, the man was gone.

Mother redoubled her vigilance and would hardly let me pee alone for the remainder of that perilous season. She had suffered too much in recent times, and the events inspired a rededication to the spiritual brand of her childhood. The Caldwell's had never been typical church folk, adhering instead to the iron fervor of Father's doctrines — the peculiar prayers he would have us recite at mealtimes, and that small book of principles he read to us from. And perhaps it was these convictions that set the stiff in his spine against the event that had all Jesper aflutter: a three-day traveling revival service.

Pastor Ashley and The Cowboy Apostles had conscripted a fine poster that adorned many of the windows in Main Street's storefronts. Spelled out in cream western bubble letters, the incoming show promised true and holy worship of a doctrinally-sound nature, spiritual wonderments, a healing prayer, and for the young souls, song and rope tricks that would illustrate profound biblical truths. Mother desired these like a sugar-dusted pound cake, and she would have her treat categorically.

Surely, she persuaded, rubbing the chapped rawhide of Father's heels, her man could appreciate the accomplished twirling of a lasso, if not these other offerings. Surely, Heaven is too grand to fit into any one guise. But Mother's efforts only stoked Father's bitterness and his resolve hardened like cement. The Caldwell's, Father thundered, were forbidden to patronize such apostasy. Yea, in protest, we would not show our faces in Jesper all week.

That was that, and Father was law.

Father resigned his evenings with drink. This, Mother afforded him, for we all grieve in our own ways. As for me, I took my sorrows out on the pigeons with my BB gun. That is, until one day when I only grazed the eyeball of a bird and it fell to the ground and hopped along in misery. I followed it about our yard, and every time it jerked its head, out flew a crystalline droplet of blood like the turnover of a lawn sprinkler. I put it down with the butt of my gun, and after that, turned to shooting towers of Father's empties.

The day before Pastor Ashley's final tent service, Mother wore a fetching cotton dress — a burst of paisley and color not seen on her in months. She fixed Father grits and collards and butchered her favorite fowl to prepare him a splendid fried chicken. We never ate with such luxury — the very venture of it was risk, and Father's temper more arsenic than amethyst. The Caldwell's persisted in a state of debilitating lack despite the antiquated luxuries around us, and the apparent success of our farm as Father leased new land and hired-on extra laborers, stretching our gruel and demanding we forever patch the patches on our secondhand clothes.

Mother set him in his leading chair and scooted him into the banquet she had prepared. Country western on the turntable too, Loretta Lynn. Kissing him on the smooth of his widow's peaks, she leaned her arms around to cut his food such that her pale, freckled bosom pillowed his neck. As for me, I did as instructed and popped his beer, then slurped the froth off like he liked. Soon, his second beer. His third. We sat with him while he drank, quiet of course, and he talked his nonsense, making a spider's web of connections between forest rovings, his better life before we bound him to earthly labor amongst such spiritual impotents, and his most memorable hands at cards. He took his fourth beer with the ball game on TV. He took his fifth with the paper. He took his sixth and seventh to his bed, and by the time they were drained to the last warm drop, he had drifted into the cavernous slumber of a tranquilized bear.

Mother summoned me back to the kitchen table. She asked if I wanted to attend Pastor Ashley's final service with her the following evening. I did, of course, I told her, but Father had forbidden it. But Mother had some mischief in mind. She removed her house shoes and fetched her sewing basket from the cupboard. Milling around inside, she selected the largest needle. Then she went to the bathroom and returned with several containers of dental floss. Bidding me hush with a blithesome finger to her lips, she, a magician of the old floorboards and their telltale creaks, noiselessly crept upstairs.

An hour or two later, Mother returned. I had occupied myself in the kitchen with a new whittling project on a block of oak, and a small mountain of shavings surrounded my foiled ambitions. I had intended it to be a tree, but somehow my unskilled hands had produced a figurine much more like a bird.

Come upstairs and see, Mother said, a strange look on her face, like she was fleshing out two distant locations at once. Come and see what I have done.

I followed her, sleepy, for it was now past ten o'clock.

Opening her bedroom door, Mother motioned me inside. As my eyes adjusted to the dim room, I perceived Father, still conked atop the bed and snoring something horrid. His muscular arms and torso and long legs were spread wide and flat and were clearly outlined by the topsheet, which was pulled up to just under his chin.

As I neared the bed, I beheld something neon green — like long sinuous trails of ivy — traveling all around my father's frame. The offense Mother had weft came sharply into focus: with the waxed dental floss she had deployed the skill of her hands — she had sewn him into the mattress. So fine were her close stitches with the sturdy floss separating his spread-eagle limbs — even tacking deftly between each finger — that she had rendered the topsheet as taut as a gale-blown sail, and Father immobile beneath it, until she cut him loose in her own good time.

Outside the bedroom, Mother handed me my backpack. We crept downstairs where she retrieved the keys to Father's truck and a few other sundries. To Jesper we would go — to Pastor Ashley and The Cowboy Apostles — for the final service the following day.

In the motel room, Mother helped herself to one of several beers she'd stolen from Father's stash. She paced the widow's walk of that filthy carpet and snickered incessantly — the nervous release of months of rigid dread and bottomless loss. After another beer, she finally sat down and flipped on the TV, and we watched *The Lucy Show* in a cloud of floral-printed bedspreads and ruffled pillows.

The following morning, the room was empty. I found Mother outside behind the wheel of the truck. She was crying, and I feared she'd lost her nerve. But sighting me, she regained composure and cracked the window to call out that I join her. I drew my knees up to my chest and counted the broken rungs in the air conditioning vent. Wiping her eyes, she told of listening that morning to a broadcast of Pastor Ashley's sermon on the radio, and we were, she swore, in for a real treat come five o'clock.

We ate soggy waffles and drank powdered Tang for breakfast in the motel's hospitality room.

We caught *The Sound of Music* in the local theatre and my cheap seat broke and I wanted to be a puppetress more than anything in the world.

We ate riblets and potato rolls for lunch in the corner booth of a diner. A poster in the window, pinned a little aggressively over Pastor Ashley's, announced Jesper's next coming attraction—a traveling freakshow with strongmen and knife swallowers. A woman who could read minds. A house of mirror and shadow. And a hairless bear.

The final service was held in an open-air tent erected over the Mayor's large corral on the outskirts of town. Though we arrived early, the extravaganza's finale had already drawn the bulk of Jesper's residents, and they milled around in their laundered coveralls and prim Sunday dresses. Pastor Ashley and The Cowboy Apostles were nowhere in sight, though a stage had been set in advance with a drumset, pedal steel, double bass, and a dobro. Cowhand mutts slunk about inside the tent, sniffing at the red-and-white checkered tablecloths that held the potluck. And the flies—Heaven, the flies—they swarmed like a true biblical plague about the abundance of tin-foil-covered barbecue and the mysteries of side dishes in sealed pastel Tupperware.

At once, the crowd gave in to clamor. A cloud of dust had kicked up coming from Jesper's Main Street. At the head of the party rode Pastor Ashley. He was an enormous man even at a distance, with a long flowing beard that the wind split over his leather-vested belly. He carried the confidence everlasting of a prosperous tycoon, one hand on the reins while the other waved a white cowboy hat above his head.

About him rode The Cowboy Apostles—two twin buckaroos in breeches and black shirts to his left, a buxom woman in a black trench coat with tight red curls to his right, and a lanky sawtoothed man in a grey suit just behind who was a dead ringer for Sam Elliot. All Jesper cheered as Pastor Ashley and The Cowboy Apostles took a victory lap around the tent before reining up at the entrance. There, Pastor Ashley reared his horse a final time, eclipsing the sun with the great expanse of his head. He hollered out a good God bless ye, then spat a great arc, and his chaw did land in a brown puddle at my feet.

The revivalists gave over their reins to eager volunteers and took immediately to the stage. Pastor Ashley balanced the dobro on that belly, while the twins occupied the drumset and pedal steel. The woman stood behind the double bass and the gunslinger produced a fiddle. So arranged, the group launched into a rousing bluegrass rendition of "Come Thou Fount of Every Blessing." I held Mother's worn hand. Tears rindled her face. She seemed transported to the very throne room of Heaven. All of Jesper stomped the dirt. Yea, the rhythm was effectual, and our swaying limbs said so, but the sound of the dobro, badly out of tune, and the feline screech of the gunslinger's fiddle, caused me unpardonable offense. Before the first song had subsided, the Mayor ascended the stage. At an encouraging nod from Pastor Ashley—a consecration that all but sealed the Mayor the next election—he raised high a thigh of barbecue chicken and commenced a series of fancy steps.

Another song followed, a slow one, for all needed a breather. There were no chairs so most stood—to sit was a shame. Mother wore a look— elation, surprise, sweat—like she'd successfully made her own mother's sweet potato pie.

Pastor Ashley's sermon went short, much to all there gathered's surprise. A chair had been brought onstage, and instead of cantering around as he had the prior nights, he sat for his address. This night, he said—quietly, rumbly, palms on his knees, then stroking the length of his beard from chin to tip—is a night for reflection. What had Jesus Christ, the original desperado, said about leaving off your trappings and following Him? Why, even little children are welcome to join the Promised Land Posse.

Pastor Ashley leaned back in the chair, and it creaked like an attic floor about to give way. He then glanced toward the periphery of the stage. From my vantage, I perceived one of the twin Cowboy Apostles there in the shadows, crouching behind the double-bass case. At the ready, he held a small blonde boy, five at most, just above the elbows.

The twin then whispered some harsh word into the boy's ear and released him. The boy rushed forward, frightened and bewildered, toward the middle of the stage, no doubt looking for his mother. There, Pastor Ashley absorbed the boy like a schoolyard bully does his pitiful challenger, whipping him up and around his broad shoulders, and when the boy landed, facing the audience on the revivalist's knee, it was with swirling eyes and a panting mouth, like he'd just toured the stars and spheres.

Pastor Ashley slapped the boy heavy on the back and guffawed and all Jesper joined in the comedy. As I seethed, Mother nudged me with her elbow. She was holding Pastor Ashley's great white hat. Circulating among the crowd, the ten-gallon overflowed with offerings; it said much to me about how to make a buck.

Tonight, Pastor Ashley said, immediately following the service, he and the Cowboy Apostles would depart, head deep into Texas, then New Mexico, Arizona, and on to the great, godless California, land of the fruits and the nuts. Wouldn't it be something, he intimated in his powerfully low rumble, if when the Cowboy Apostles arrived at the next tent, at the next town, it was with such a great cloud of witnesses? Why, this was how the twins had joined—they were attendees at a rally in Auburn. And this spitting image for Sam Elliot? He hailed from a recent service in Lynchburg, Tennessee.

I looked closer at Pastor Ashley's teeth while he spoke, studying the wide smile he cast about when making his appeal. Glimmer and shimmer, his orderly, pearled rows were out for admiration, like they were parading the arena in the Westminster Dog Show. He may have brushed well—he may have gargled with a dash of Clorox—or bent his lips to some sacred fountain to rinse—but I'll be damned if those sharp front ones couldn't have doubled for bullets.

—Got a hitch in your giddyup? Pastor Ashley thundered. He'd lifted the child onto his shoulders and begun his galloping tour around the stage. Feeling the lassitude of idle hands? Well, the Kingdom of God is conscripting. If the spirit moves you, saddle up. We ride on the Almighty's business.

This concluded Pastor Ashley's invitation. When he had the whole crowd fired-up and ready to march on the gates of Hell, he stopped dead center on the stage and bowed his head. As the crowd hushed, he commenced the resonant hum of a venerable melody until all joined him in song—an acapella version of "Amazing Grace"—which doubled as a blessing for the food. While we sang, the man to my right nudged me. He held a black hat, the one the gunslinger had worn, and it was filled with money too. When I handed it to my mother, she produced her small, pearled purse and donated a second time.

The food line was long, and I excused myself to climb a set of nearby bleachers. I saw John Mosley underneath that metal castle, and more importantly, saw an occasion to sidle up to my crush. He was kneeling, his back to me, and when I peered over his shoulder, I perceived he was fiddling with a naked Barbie. He had the doll sitting down, legs spread in a wide, white-v, and had brushed back the interminable blond tornado of her coarse hair into something that seemed respectable. In his other hand he held an unwrapped condom. I knelt next to him, and he handed me the cream rubber and then sat back on his butt and searched the grounds around him. Coming up with a long, bare twig, he took the rubber back from me. He then unrolled it and poked the twig into the condom's wider end. I held Barbie's arm as he wedged it into her hand. We set her before us and admired our handiwork.

—Yea, let us imagine her future, I said, awash in the sense this tableau carried some important meaning. Behold as Barbie runs naked through the fields, capturing the glory specimens of Heaven with her butterfly net. Here, she is with child; here, she gives it away, only for Heaven to return her all that was lost, though cured of its ills and marked for the Divine, for her body is a secret kingdom, and Heaven always guides.

—Why do you Caldwell's talk like that? John Mosley asked.

—Like what? I asked, as my fervor wore off, and I did then cover up my twitching lip and did then fear I flushed.

—Like you're from some old spooky fairytale.

Rather than try out a clever rationale for my trance, for I wasn't feeling very romantic after that affront, I mumbled up some excuse and beat a hasty retreat to the main tent. There, I spied Pastor Ashley outside in intimate conversation with my mother. Hands on his hips, he threw back his head and belly-laughed at some sparkling remark she'd apparently just made. Mother then clasped her hands across the pretty paisley dress she'd worn as if pleading for something. I felt revolt in my chest, like I must defend her from a house of booby traps. But when I started over, she shot me a look like I was blowing her cover.

And so I went in search of supper. The food was true bounty. I filled up my plate once, then again, washing the helpings down with waxy Dixie cups of fruit punch. When mother finally returned inside the tent, she walked straight to me and said we must go, and now. It was nearing eight o'clock and the sun had long set and different folks in Jesper were taking their turns with the instruments on the stage, all with far superior ability to the Cowboy Apostles.

On the short drive home, Mother didn't say a word about the service. I asked if she was hungry since she hadn't eaten as far as I could tell, but she told of tasting something much more satisfying than barbecue. While I did not believe such a thing possible, I kept quiet out of respect for her devotion. We turned up the drive to our house and Mother parked the truck. She handed me my backpack and the keys.

—Go on in, she said. Then, wait, here, take this. From the glovebox, she fished out an old pocketknife. Go upstairs and cut him loose.

—Why me? I pleaded. He'll whip me. He's gonna rage.

—He won't. Not this time. He knows it was me who did it.

—Aren't you coming in?

—I have to attend to something.

—You're going back to Jesper? I asked. But the question was stale bread even as the words sounded from my mouth.

She sat silent for a good long while, and when it arrived her response was assured.

—I have to tend to myself.

She then pulled her hair into a ponytail, bound it. In the truck's dome light, her curls did look flaky as a cinnamon dusted cruller. She leaned over and gave me a long hug.

—Now go see to your father. He's probably sullied himself.

Mother quit the truck and threw the keys out into the yard. I followed her as far as the driveway's edge as she continued walking on to Jesper. Though I called out, she did not look back.

Sometimes you pass the cowboy hat; sometimes you cut and run, live to squabble another day. Sometimes you trade a stone for a lasso. Sometimes you sit with your father, and all is strangely resolved. And sometimes, you go camping and invite a threat into your bedroll, and while Heaven watches with the assurance of ordination, let go of your will and spit in your palm and shake.

Reader, I include now the telling of my final remove at the hands of the Nightingale, to the most severe and enduring of my sheds, when the Mother found me after the storm in a trance of Heaven, naked and bleeding and beholding the newborn Boy in his cradle while also writing in my little books.

BOOK VII

LOST YEARS to a SHED
& THE OPEN ROOF
& THE WORMS
& THE BEGINNINGS of DESCENT
& THE ADVENT of the VULTURES
& A HEAVENLY REMOVE

Heartless sun.

The windstorm splintered off the roof of this shed, blew it asunder. Steady in decay, scorched by the heat, I wished only for quick expiration. I thrummed my fingers against the baked dirt and hummed snatches of the hymns I'd heard so many years before at Jesper's tent revival service. I replayed every event of my life I could remember until they bled together into mush. But most of all, I yearned for the cool soothe of the grave.

Countless days, perhaps a thousand, they'd left me in this shed. Not a soul had graced me, not even the Son. A nameless saint daily lowered my scant food and water over the lip of the beams, and with a ragged blanket I did effort to shield myself from the heat.

The worms below, sightless and pale—at last these gravedig-gers answer my resounding. A legion of them emerge from the earth, prodding over each other en masse, testing the air for predators. They swarm over me like fleshy sea algae, threading my fingertips, braceleting my wrists, squiggling over the rash of my wounds. They plug in my nostrils and ears and explore the dry depths of my mouth.

As the body worsens, apportion of the senses lengthens. This shed has prepared me for new language. I whisper my legacy and receive theirs in communion. Soil churns beneath me during the night's darkest hours. The worms converge their efforts, carving out the earth to steal me away to some great subterranean dwelling. I had resolved my future long before. And still, death had not found me. Perhaps this burial might bring respite.

But when the sun breaks that dawn, and the worms depart to the cool of their tunnels, my face and shriveling limbs still protrude above the surface. There, a lone visitor arrives and perches on the edge of my roofless shed — my bird — sulking its head low into the middle of its chest.

Eat, my vulture charges.

I open my mouth to feed and feel the vulture release the raw cake of a lump. I chew but the taste is unwholesome to me. Spewing it out, I find the nourishment is the harvest of my own foot; the smallest of my toes.

A dozen more vultures land on the edge of the shed. With these adversaries sighted, myriads of worms resurface and swarm over me anew, a fleshy thresher of slime and soil. Other worms below renew their fervor, and I sink deeper into the earth.

And then it begins to rain.

The vultures sweep in like a tourbillon, methodical and ruthless, sundering the worms with beak and claw. The burned reek of blood overwhelms. And what is this—do my senses deceive? The worms have deployed their Goliath. The thick champion tunnels from the dirt between my legs, and lashing about, constricts the powerful wings of one vulture. With its gaping maw, it bites off the bird's head. But the worms prove a diminished regiment, and the remaining vultures butcher this champion into piecemeal. Likewise, the vultures do sunder the balance of my shed's companions—my deliverers—my tormentors.

Gripping my feet and ankles, hands and arms, even forehead, hair, and sorry lip with their talons, the vultures excise me from burial and depart with me to the sky. I have never known this sensation—the sensation of absolute weightlessness—of disagency—as each joint of my body is gripped and rendered docile.

The vultures carry me to the city in the clouds — the same city I had witnessed in the inlet with the Son. Our sun is but a single jewel in its walls, and no jewel greater than any other. I look for comfort among the terrible red faces of my vultures but find no consolation; only their beady, black eyes intent on the star before us.

They will carry me to our sun's innermost. I will incubate there. And after I have received the investment and instruction of Heaven — called and awakened — my spirit will return to Acacia, to the Pear House of the Prophetess Mother Nightingale.

Dear Valorized Reader,

Bound by vow that I would not transcribe the experience of my instruction in Heaven, the reader must allow the absence of this portion of my testimony. Yet, as a warning to counter those competing accounts which privilege certain features—the manifestation of a bright light, the presence of guiding martyrs, the storehouses which hold the stock to restore our earthly bodies, the mansions built in luxury in proportion to one's earthly virtue—discard them all. Heaven is the birthplace of war and the violent take it by force.

BOOK VIII

*RETURNED to the PEAR HOUSE
& POWER in the WORD
& THE DESTRUCTION of the PEAR
HOUSE and the DECAY
of the NIGHTINGALE
& THE VESSEL of HEAVEN*

Earthly sense returned to my body—I was bound by iron chains in a spare room of the Pear House, at the opposite end of the great hall from the Nightingale's childhood bedroom and her current quarters. Empty of furniture, of ornamentation, this room's purpose was reformatory. I had returned from the clouds. My skin and worm wounds had healed completely. I was no longer Petra the Wretched, but the harbinger of Heaven, bound only to Its will, an open channel of vision and reality. My lip set its temper.

The men with rakes outside felt the sensation as my vision carried forth to a forest ablaze with laurel leaves. I dropped to my knees on the old hardwood, and lowered my face to their crackles, and brayed out the spirits of my lungs, stomach, and bowels.

The grounds of Acacia billowed as Heaven's scepter met me in the room and touched the earth. The walls of the Pear House ruptured at the foundation and I watched as real cracks ran from the crown moulding to the baseboards. Shingles shook loose and cascaded to the garden like waxed playing cards. The furniture tipped. Chasms unfastened about the grounds as easily as two boys tear apart a paper doll. Water from the inlet flooded into the grounds.

And when all earthly sense retained and I sat amongst such devastation, I found my shackles had shorn loose from the walls. I did then dance down the hall and out of the broken doorframe of the Pear House, my chains whipping through the air as light as tinsel.

As I intimated, my lengthy time in Heaven had refreshed my body. Bulbs no longer protruded from my legs, nor did the sores do up my face and arms, nor did the worm's nibbles nor the vulture's talons mark me. My limbs were as lean and muscular as an Olympic runner and my hair faultless and flowing as wind-treated wheat.

But the Prophetess Mother had not fared so well during my internment and my restoration. She had languished in her bedroom. In proportion to my healing, Heaven siphoned her in peels and layers. A brutal topography, her hair receded, yes, to the back of her head. Her skin burbled with sores, and she had reduced beyond what seemed possible, as though Heaven had stuffed a hose down her throat and Hoovered out her innards.

As the men with rakes surrounded me, naked on our grounds, the severed chains a testimony to my favor—as the women with jars each reached inside and extinguished their flame with fingertips—as the water from the Lake O' The Pines muddied the soil beneath my feet—I marveled at the elasticity of Divine favor.

A tongue belonged first to a seer, then to an old woman, then to a husk of moaning cold meat. Christen that tongue with vinegar and spite. Squeeze its wilting dryness until it cracks like a potato chip. Extract a final word.

In my periphery, a man with a rake drew closer, resolved in his allegiance to the Prophetess Mother. When he lunged and gripped my naked arm, he fell to the ground and gave up the ghost.

Who would then test me? None among them gathered, not this day. I was no longer Petra the Wretched. I was the vessel of Heaven. And I had come to set the captives free.

BOOK IX

THE RESTORATION of the NIGHTINGALE at my HAND & HER AVATAR TRUSTED YET & THE GENESIS of the ORB

But regency was, for a time, postponed. For under my patient care — and with a Heavenly storehouse of mercy I could never hope to rationalize — the Mother was tended with salves, tinctures, and the wisdoms of my herbcraft (which she herself had taught me), as well as massages, ice baths, and even intercession. Through me the Nightingale's tongue thus revivified, as its thick yellow pus and black fuzz thinned, then surrendered to health. The organ, pink as a piece of supermarket salmon, again exited her mouth to speak with a timbre tenuous as ash. She asked to be fed bone broth with an egg spoon. She asked after the hand mirror hanging from a gutterspike nail beside her vanity. Her brittle bones restored their flesh. Her hair returned in long tresses, though gone was the mercurial red and she was gray entire. Her decimation rewound as fast as a videocassette.

The Son escorted her to the front porch of the Pear House. Steadying herself with her rake, she greeted the assembled flock, even me, Petra the Chosen Bird. A portion of the men bowed their heads in deference. A few of our women moved their jarred candles in front of their hearts. But it was a gesture drained of meaning for those many who looked first to me.

The Prophetess Mother then called me to join her on the stairs, which I did in my own good time. Surely, here she'd try some stunt and sing of my healing arts as the soil-caked spikes of her rake swept toward my temple. But no, she embraced me. Her pinions were so firm I could scarcely move. Her lips circled, and descended, enveloping my face in the soft bedding of her grey hair before planting tightly into the meat of my cheek. There was no wet. No nick, nor teeth, nor telltale testing prick, nor running of the blood.

Come to me this evening, she whispered. And her voice was light, and mirthful, and rippling with urgent music. I wondered — where was the plot? Where had she hidden the violent shock of her snare? I tuned in my faculties to detection, eyeing her and certain saints with vigilance, but she moved away from me and waved again to the gathered crowd, showing them her restoration — her arms and legs and transmuted hair, even sticking out her pink tongue.

I quit the porch and strode to the chapel to pray for discernment, for she was a high school mischief maker, and through my hand, I wondered if she again held the key to Heaven's liquor cabinet.

Come twilight, yet. As the feast dishes were cleared from the picnic tables outside, as the children were sung to sleep, as the saints reclined in their chairs, she took in time to her bedroom.

I knocked and she bade me enter. Her candlelit bedroom sulked like a rebellious child, and in the midst of it all the Mother leaned into the abundant throw pillows populating her bed, atop a pink chenille coverlet besotted with charred, caramel holes from spilled ash. She held her favorite pipe in one hand, and it lilted cherry smoke to the ceiling like the hypnotic censers of a scaly old cathedral.

I sat down in the plush easy chair she indicated for me, near the ashtray, near a woodcut bird statue atop the TV, amidst the luxurious cages she kept always for all kinds of fowl.

We began with benign pleasantries, asking after our mutual enjoyment of the dinner, for young Fleur's majesty in the kitchen never ceased to astonish, especially with the unusual herbs her young Boy, just five years old, managed to source from the thicket. The Mother then invited me to join her on the bed. I crossed the room and did then set myself beside her, kneading my hands involuntarily, then alternately finding them in fists.

But there came no word about my expectation for this visit—
that is, my miraculous bodily healing after my torturous season
with the worms, or hers, or this new and tangible regard that
Acacia paid to me, which must have given her all the pleasure
of a heat rash.

No, instead she wished to hear simple stories; stories about my
time before Acacia, all the way back to the Jesper of my childhood. I had to crawl across the mattress when she asked me to,
to position myself against the headboard beside her, so that she
could hear me properly in her stronger right ear over the jokes
and audience laughter of a new program named *Late Night with
David Letterman,* and the soft wisps of her hair did brush against
my bare shoulders as the host onscreen flashed his smile and she
reached across me for her dented gold Zippo and a fresh pinch
of cherry tobacco from the bedside jar.

And I did then open up my account for her, drawing on that
uncanny wellspring of compassion I had in her caretaking. The
Mother relished the telling of my father's fervor for holy words
and all the absurdity of the Caldwell's devotions with the dice,
the book, the bell. She cackled at the report of the small loaves
of our table, spilling her ash about the bedspread; a laughter

which shook her small frame so violently I thought she'd void her bladder. She delighted at the account of Pastor Ashley and The Cowboy Apostles — of my father sewn into the bed, especially — and she seemed equally awed at my mother's moxie, like she'd just peered into the inner workings of a jack-in-the-box and the springs and sprockets had said something truly revolutionary about the universe. But she delighted most of all in one story during that year of danger — after my mother had returned from her evangelical misstep — when I had the privilege of joining my daddy for his card game in Jesper.

Dear Subspinous Reader,

I hope that you will permiss me to break the margins of my little books and enliven for you this special narrative which so delighted the Nightingale, and which did mark a particular season of my life with a rare jewel — a bond with my fallen patriarch — for it is a memory, a season of memories, really, like a long field of a nearly identical flower, which I have relived often, and drafted, and dreamed of again, and again, and again such that it has now become a dream-object. I hold it up to the light for you and ask you to examine it for bloody signs and fitful visions. I expect you will find none, and so here perhaps you will read me as just the curious, spunky, eager-to-please child I could have remained had Heaven not remained me to its keep.

The dream-object, the artifact, as I transcribe it for the first time for my archive, is this:

ARKANSAS—THE CALDWELL FARM, IN THE EARLY WARM OF SPRING, 1966.

It took her a choice two years, but at last my mother returned from her apostolic stunt in Pastor Ashley's circus, donned afresh in mourning dress with a little tweed suitcase in her hands. Her time away with the revivalists, but more importantly back in the big wide world, introduced to Ava Caldwell unquenchable fantasy. She wanted her own fowl gun and a sack of fine White Lily flour. She wanted a car ride to the Florida coast. She wanted a permanent nail of mistletoe above her bedroom door. But Heaven delivered her a millstone of grief, and she found her way back to us to weep day-after-day beside the grave of my sister, the stone. Though my father held the screen door wide for her without a smidge of discernible scorn, the distance of planets now separated them. Soon, she grew ill. My father noticed the change in the pre-dawn glimmers as we gathered around the table. Your skin looks awful, Ava, he said. You've gone yellow, like cat piss. And yellow she was, for she was through and through jaundiced.

Doctor came and went and sent her to bedrest. Mother could not walk, and thusly could not work. Only one pair of hands in the farmhouse remained. Big in my britches now, I tended the laundry, managed the bread, and kept our kitchen shipshape.

The first Friday, Father missed it with his sour grumbling, and a sixer of Bud Heavies, and a sharp kick against the wall that sent the tip of his boot through the plaster. But by the second week, his itch grew too great. He would endure me for his weekly card game in nearby Jesper. Why he did not leave me home is uncertain, though perhaps he suspected my mother's worldly influence. Or perhaps he wished for me to appreciate my privileged station under the shadow of his wing.

I tried on several prized dresses for our excursion but settled on a pastel pink Easter number. I then exorcised the rat of my hair and pinned it down with plastic butterfly barrettes. I spit on my shoes and gave them a last buff with the edge of the tablecloth when he wasn't looking. And I then bade my mother goodbye in the downstairs guestroom. Her smile, straddling death's threshold, blessed me stay safe, even if in my father's company.

Father sat quiet on our short drive, his concentration always a ritual, as the truck's radio fuzzed in and out like a loose lightbulb. He wore a distinct hat to cards, a Stetson, winged with the David Allan Coe bend.

Near Jesper, Father discovered the cottonmouth, mature and thick, noiselessly coiling about his boots in the well of the truck. His swiftness shattered the quiet. He gripped the serpent by the tail as it burrowed under the bench seat, and his stubborn made no concession. Father wrenched. Like the extension of a bullwhip, the snake stretched the distance of the cab, fangs and hiss traveling past my face, past the little silver door lock that looked like a rounded tombstone, and out the open window before Father's counter-yank disposed it to the highway. His cigarette kept its going and he dragged it to the filter.

The temperature reached apogee; a high-blaze to strip you of dignity. Put Father's way, this made Hell a temptation. Heaven gave us weathermen, he muttered as sweat split upon his eyelashes, to make governments seem truthful.

Law tagged us as we rolled into Jesper. The officer set to his business, but Father knew him and sneaked in a question after the man's old Catahoula hound. That got law talking. After a sit, we drove on with good wishes for the game ahead.

Our destination was the VFW, housed in an old Victorian estate with a welcoming front porch off Main Street. The building was raised on short-stilts to guard against flooding and showed an elegant dotage; a century of happenings in the porous siding and crusted windows.

This game today, Father said as we ascended the stairs, is for the nine dimes. I had that much, twice maybe, in my piggy bank. I told Father so and he paused with a marvelous thrill in his eyes and withdrew his dice from his pocket—one black and one white—and cast them on the porch. The dice careened about the splinters the way a cheetah chases a gazelle, tight on the turns, skedaddling up against a beaten rocking chair and an ash tray in heavy use, before petering out on the old, chipped boards. Father had chuckled when he threw, but whatever consequences he derived from that impulse numerology soured him like the news of a bounced check.

The grand parlor inside the VFW was in use for an event for Jesper's old timers. To the left sat a waist-high stage decorated with flag bunting. Atop it, a man entertained on a chestnut player piano, his body bent over the keys like a hard-right turn. A fat Border Collie slumbered at his feet. Rows of copper aluminum folding chairs faced the stage, filled with perspiring whitehairs. Though the rhythm presented strong argument for dancing, the attendees were as still and bitter as blackstrap molasses.

Father's game was hosted in a room upstairs. He led me up to his weekly confederates: five men and a single woman. One of these men had just served Secret Service for our President, Lyndon Johnson. Another painted houses with a treated chemical product that wouldn't chip for fifteen years, guaranteed. One had pawned his child's bike for a bus ticket from Bentonville. The lady was named Thessalonia and she suffered rectal cancer and had invented something or other for farm equipment.

Save my promise to remain in the building, Father gave me leash to explore. He said he might be an hour, may be a dozen. Everything depended on the length of luck and Heaven.

Good fortune, Daddy, I said.

From the back of the main first-floor room, I listened to the man playing piano for a good while. He was a jaunty player, and I admired the strong strikes in his play. Woefully, though, in a long pause between his songs, I released an ill-timed cough. A small head full of PEEPS-yellow curlers turned at me first. A man across her aisle with a high starched collar gave me the stares. A bloated woman in a pink muumuu looked like she'd roast me for Sunday lunch. Before the next song kicked up, I removed myself and went exploring.

At the end of a long hallway off the main room, I found a door ajar and pushed it open with my shoe. Streaming in from the opposing window, flares of light reflected off dozens of hulking, lustered-wood frames, rounded at the top like rainbows. I was bewildered, and awestruck too, like I'd found the entryway to Oz. But a moment later the room clarified—it was a storage space—a boneyard for antique jukeboxes.

Before I left, I staked my territory, writing my full name in cursive in the thick dust of the nearest glass face. I then peered through the clean portal of my signature and at the mechanics inside. A silver robot arm was poised mid-extraction, but the 45 pinched in its metal claw, this still remained within the rotary. Whatever song was next I'd never know. I would still like to know.

Next, a locked room in the VFW. A second one too.

I turned the next doorknob to reveal a bare room, not much larger than a utility closet. Inside, two boys, kindergarten or so, faced each other. Jeans unzipped, each held their peewee like a showdown at high noon. At an unknown signal, they spun in circles, urinating.

I returned upstairs to the card game. Father sat at the table with a full jar of Muscadine wine, a look in his eyes like he wished to light his cards on fire, while a large pile of money rested in the center of the table. I lay my head against a velveteen throw pillow with yellow tassels in the corner and rested—though I never fell asleep—for an unspoken vow of the smaller set is never concede your slumber.

When I opened my eyes, Thessalonia had misplaced one of her shoes under the table, high-heeled and Bloody-Mary-red. Father toed the tipped over pump. Soon, he removed his boot and scraped off his dirty white sock and slipped his foot inside. His toes managed the shoe's contours, but his chapped heel bulged too grotesque to fit.

The table turned and was now at Father's mercy. Only three competitors remained. The witching hour had passed. Soon, I drifted off beyond excuse.

Orders like the bark of a hostile dog, menacing and sharp, returned me to consciousness. Rough hands hauled me to my feet. A duo of robbers had pushed their way into the card room. A stubby silver pistol was pointed at my head and suggested to the table that they all had a choice—do right by me or wrong. I would bear the consequence of the table's wisdom.

The pot was rendered to the robbers' burlap sack. Father delivered his wallet and the watch he'd won. Thessalonia's gaudy, deco, costume jewelry went in too. Then both of her expensive heels, kicked off Father's feet.

When the room emptied of the robbers, Father rushed me down to the porch to watch them pile into a traffic-cone-orange Gremlin parked up the street. The lead bandit, already in the seat of the car, wielded the sack of bounty in triumphant summons to the second thief, not far behind. The whitehairs remained seated in the main room behind us, attuned to their concert, oblivious to the theft, but our clamor to the porch drew the attention of the piano player.

Pushing past Father, the player produced a long-barreled revolver from beneath his smart, black duster. He demanded we hush. He began to hum. He then leveraged the gun, paused, and let fire a single shot. The fleeing thief received his just desserts as, mere steps from the Gremlin, his head ripped open like a flimsy blouse. The player cocked the gun again and laid waste to the second bandit seated in the driver's seat.

Father and I returned home with his winnings. He took to his workshop and made me swear I'd leave my sickly mother and the house alone. I obeyed for a good while, busying myself near the woodpile where a garden serpent sunned. I grabbed it by its tail, like Father had the cottonmouth, and whipped it round a tree, breaking its skull against the hard bark with the tight rapt of a snare drum.

I thought it couldn't hurt to just peek in on Mother. I snuck up and cupped my hands against the window of the downstairs bedroom where she rested. Peering inside, I felt all hallelujah squeal out of me like a helium balloon, for my mother was laid out on top of the comforter as if for her viewing. Her hair was pulled upwards into a bun and tightly pinned, and she wore her best dress: a nightmare-pitch, lace Victorian gown, ornamented with a thousand clasps and cloth button closures. Her skin retained its terrible pallor, like thoroughly beaten egg yolks. Beside her on the nightstand on a plate of fine white china sat a thick cut of porterhouse, split open in the middle, seeping juices.

A horsefly bothered the room. An irritating buzz. It circled my mother's head and came to rest on her cold rouged cheek. I wept and banged the glass with dirty palms. Mother's face did not twitch, nor did her resolute eyelids, nor her lips, hushful. But her hand. Her hand alighted with the explosive charge of a revolver, descending to bludgeon the fly. Only then did her lashes flutter open as she divined the mash of carapace in her palm.

Father's voice returned to me the fear of Heaven. He strode toward me with discipline in mind, sliding out his belt from the waistband of his pants. But in the moment before he swept me up and I received my tanning, I beheld my mother lick the guts from her palm. Eyes on the ceiling, Ava Caldwell chewed mournfully.

& BOOK IX
(CONTINUES):

Disoriented, I woke alone in the Nightingale's bed. Outside, truck doors slammed, and I could make out eager voices. The night had gone long, and amidst the expanse of that comforter, I hardly recalled its end — only that after the sharing of so much legacy, I had bridged sleep next to Salome, my face nuzzled into the sleeve of her burned-out-velvet kimono, as she stroked my hair and softly gasped at the prescient horrors of *Dynasty* on her small TV.

I made my way downstairs and toward the ruckus in the yard. A group of the men with rakes had just returned from a Farm and Tractor Supply in some town a ways off and were busy unloading bags of concrete, racks of paving stones, drainage pipes, stacks of immense metal panels (each nearly fourteen feet in height), and scores of smooth lumber beams from the old logging truck belonging to Acacia. Marvelously elated, the Nightingale stood in white Keds in the middle of a thick puddle of mud at the rear of the truck, burbling mirthfully under her breath as she made marks on a clipboard. I joined her, announced myself when she didn't notice, and made clear she ought to explain this intervention.

— Each object of our desire should be like a garden bed left fallow, she said, and nary yearned for in its befores and afters, or its heretofores, or woebegones, or even in the everlastings, for is it not so that everything is perfect in its time?

She took a step toward the truck as though she might unload a heavy beam herself. But I grasped her by the arm and stayed her. I had little patience for parables, and I asked her to speak plainly. And there I learned of her plans for a new structure in Acacia, distinct in its architecture, set apart from our other buildings. She had carried the idea close to her bosom since her first days in Acacia as a little girl; from before her inception as Prophetess.

— In this auspicious era of Acacia's reconstruction, she said, we were richly tilled for such an edifice, this deepest of offerings: her orb.

The orb — a building of spherical dimensions, a half-dome, laid with a sturdy concrete foundation and paneled on its inner and outer walls with multiple layers of the glistening sheet metal. She drew for me a sketch as we stood side-by-side in the mud. There would be no doors. No windows. No opening, save a hole, cut from its top. It was, the Nightingale informed me as she pulled me close and spit-shined away a scale of sleep caked at the corner of my eye, a place for a new kind of worship.

Dear Discerning Reader,

Never, not for a serpent's blink, did I misjudge this uneasy, unspoken truce, nor the corrupted kindnesses of the Prophetess Mother Salome Nightingale.

BOOK X

*A WALK
in the NIGHTINGALE'S GARDEN
& THE HISTORY of ACACIA,
PRESERVED HEREIN
& A ROPE SWING NAMED
the RAPTURE
& A VERY PUBLIC DALLIANCE*

As in my early days, once again the Nightingale invited me to join her on her evening walk. She exalted the men with rakes laboring in the community garden, swooping her arm in our blessing with a special vigor. We pushed past our boundaries and into the thicket. Past Acacia's decaying blue truck. Past my swimming hole fed by the inlet. The Mother skimmed dandelion's heads from their stems with the deft swing of her rake.

At her shadow, she shouted — I see you, shadow.

And her shadow spoke back to her in the echo.

Deep in the thicket, we reached a thick spate of crosshatched foliage, tall and looming as the gates of a haunted house. Moving a section of the mass aside, the Mother revealed a kind of doorway, and more, what lay beyond it — a hallowed grove. That whisper I heard on the day I arrived to Acacia — *hortus conclusus* — renewed upon my senses.

Sunlight swaddled the clearing with the golden haze of a summer pilsner. Manicured botanicals and shrubbery intersected with well-tended flowerbeds, teeming with Blackroot Daisy and lavender Winecup. Sharpened moss-covered logs set at the boundary between the thicket and the garden jutted inwards like *chevaux-de-frise*; like the thicket itself was the embattled bastille and wished to keep this hostile clearing at bay. About the garden, recently sculpted pillars of fallen sticks stood twice my stature, dotted with wiry nests for returning birds.

Had all my years of misery collapsed into this very instant? To this yielded opportunity? Was I yet still Petra the Wretched? Herein again was my chance to accomplish it. I could shove her to the grass, or level her with my shoulder, or kick her in the back and send her sprawling. I could seize the rake then fallen, raise it high, and demolish this ancient bird.

The Mother stopped in the center of her garden. Before her rested a large grey stone, flat and smooth and set as a table for two with dainty floral china and lilliputian silverware and a flare of fresh wildflowers in a carved wooden vase. She turned to me then, and Heaven's clarity did yet sound, despite the unwholesome vessel who spoke it:

— My child, she said, you can stop a bullet with your body. You can satiate the appetite of an ancient snake for a week with your body. You can soar your body for an unbroken minute out of an airplane before you perish in my garden, and I pick at you with my beak. Through what instrument do you view the world? The looking glass? Binoculars? The kaleidoscope? Is there any contest, child?

I remained silent.

Thus she went on:

—You have been my intimate. Have worshiped me. Sparred with me. Though age comes for me now, and I am infested by lice, and find calcium deposits in the whites of my eyes, still, notice that, rightly viewed, the spider veins in the flare of my nostrils, the varicosities bulging behind my knees, and the portals of these liver spots all reveal the thicket's blueprint. They offer a tractate of Heaven's final advent.

Said mapwork I perceived.

—Closer will you look here also, child: the legacy of Acacia is written in the entrails of a rodent. She flourished her hand.

In the middle of the stone table rested a jewelry tray, tarnished from age to a sultry, shadowy grey. The length of a child's forearm, its base was mirrored and the raised edges and handles were embellished with ornate curlicues. In the center of the jewelry tray rested the decaying remains of a simple field mouse. Its outer carcass had disintegrated to reveal its bitsy organs and the outlines of markedly long ribs and the blackened musculature of its hind legs. Where once were lips, mandibles of still-sculpted teeth sat peacefully locked. A lengthy tail of twenty-odd vertebrae extended from its hindquarters, set in a perfectly proportional spiral.

The Prophetess Mother then disrobed and knelt before the altar, and the tray, and its tiny prize, and when I had sat opposite her and made myself comfortable she told me for the first time the full account of the founding of Acacia. For the sake of our lineage, I heretofore dedicate a portion of my little books to recording this legacy. Should the Commotions blot us out, Acacia's genesis, at least, will be inscribed, for this is how Heaven established us:

Acacia

THE LAND

The territory of Acacia lies nearby the Lake O' The Pines, in the eastern portion of Texas, at the intersecting borders of Marion, Upshur, and Morris counties. Such that, during the early settling of said counties there arose a muddle, a confusion of boundaries. This created a no-man's land (spanning only several miles of especially inhospitable terrain), where, in effect, the bureaucratic oversight of each county considered this small crop of space always in the possession of one of its neighbors.

And though its surroundings were ultimately developed by Marion, Morris, and Upshur into fishing destinations with boating docks and campgrounds and picnic areas with sanitary facilities to host family reunions, by contrast the forbidding grounds of what would become Acacia grew more impenetrable by the year, shielded by natural foliage, which Heaven imbued with the properties of a warren, and sheltered over with a thorough canopy of branch, moss, and tangle.

Thus, the Land receded entirely from the venerated attentions of the law and evaded the dotted lines of development, save by Heaven, which descended its finger and staked this inner sanctum for Hesychasm. And thus, the Land was set apart, but how its community was established was this:

&⟩ THE FOUNDING

In the early 1920s, the male lineage of the Prophetess Mother Salome Nightingale maintained a successful trade in the logging industry. Hailing from Tennessee, Nightingale Lumber managed ventures throughout Arkansas, Mississippi, and western Louisiana, in which they operated sawmill company towns so long as the supply maintained.

As ambition branched Nightingale Lumber further west and into Texas to catch the tail years of the Bonanza Era of the Piney Woods — and as her enterprising husband was frequently called to oversee difficulties in the field or conflicts among competing interests whenever natural resources grew increasingly scarce — Jolene Nightingale, a young, new bride, wedded into the zealotry of this captain of industry, grew ill. She attributed her affliction to several events which had recently transpired during a walk in some distant woods.

On a Sunday excursion with her husband, having motored off a fair distance from the demands of office to partake in a picnic and supposed day of leisure, the couple neared the aforesaid intersection of counties. There they paused, as Mr. Nightingale wished to obsess over the outskirts of a grove of Texas pine heretofore unmolested. Abandoned yet again, Jolene ventured ahead into the forest on foot, enjoying the crisp air and the serene atmosphere, free of the brash character of the company town.

After a spell so occupied, she found herself separated from her husband. And terribly hungry—for Jolene was, at that time, with child—she digressed into a soft patch of tall fieldgrass and squatted down to relieve herself and meanwhile feast on some blackberries. Adjusting the slinky hemline of her long dress to avoid the puddle creeping around such stylish kitten heels, she sighted a luscious, exposed root among the willowing greens.

&. THE ROOT

It was not a gnarled and dirty thing, but a verdant ground-ling of pure jeweled greenish-yellow, splayed out from the dirt like spaghetti squash. Jolene leaned closer and brushed it with the back of her hand. Its skin felt like a luxurious sponge. She found it irresistible. She had no volition but to devour it. But the root, she could not release—though she planted the heels of her shoes at its base, soiling the backside of her dress with strenuous heaving—though she bludgeoned it with her forearms until bruised and bloodied—though she issued every word of damnation uttered in the presence of men from Philadelphia to San Francisco—the root remained earthed.

Had a bird then passed above, the scene below was a rich-priss snow angel, sobbing, flailing, in a trampled meadow.

The struggle only increased her craving. If she could not raise the root to her lips like a dainty bite of crème brûlée, like the treat she deserved, then she would descend her mouth to the plate. She scraped away the burial of its dirt, knelt before it, and planted her teeth on the root's surface.

Returning home that evening, Jolene Nightingale suffered. Her intestines flared like a pinball machine. She could not tolerate even quiet music. The color green proved insufferable. And above all, an unconscionable appetition possessed her. Nothing, save more of that root, would satisfy.

Jolene desired another backwoods banquet—but not a meal to be blanched, julienned, or sautéed, as were those served upon her mother's legacy plates and kept temperate with sterling cloches. She wished only for muddy Texas mulch with that bare root before her, for her teeth to churn once again that singular complexion of anise, pine nuts, and goat's milk—and this for the balance of her days, no matter how she might agonize, no matter how much her stomach might gyre like a gurgling cod.

As her obsession stretched on and on and into months, specialists treated her without any advance. Their consensus: Jolene Nightingale languished from nerves, and this was the cause of such commotions—her recent change into motherhood—for during this intervening time, Jolene's daughter, Salome Nightingale, had been born. Doctors over-patronized her, while Jolene, the squeaky wheel, labored at their patience, demanding that they, someone, anyone, identify the root; hunt it for her.

When the trips of lumberjacks yielded no results, and botany books proved deficient, and gardeners shrugged their shoulders, and the local grocers called security, Jolene's exasperation boiled over. She pursued her own course, bent on finding and feasting upon the root, and returning with a selection, to prove its existence and damn all these doubters' eyes.

❧ A RETURN TO THE THICKET

Beset by fever, Jolene Nightingale commandeered a company Ford Model A Roadster pickup truck and a handaxe, and ventured forth, her newly born daughter, Salome, set against the kickboard in a woven basket, which did provide a very distressing ride due to the pickup's spring shocks.

Retracing her husband's path as best as she was able, Jolene found herself on a route, well off the lumber road, leading to a field of muddied grass. Pressing on, her pickup stranded in the thick muck of a swamp near the Lake O' The Pines amidst the borders of Marion, Upshur, and Morris counties.

There, strapping baby Salome to her body, Jolene ventured on foot into the thicket. Alligator, boar, black bear, wildcat, and serpent regarded them alike, but like Daniel in the den of lions, their hungry mouths were sewn shut by the will of Heaven. Likewise affected by such Divine assurance, Jolene nary felt the tearing of her skin and bodice, nor was she upset by the deep sinking of her shoes in the morass where they went abandoned, nor by the ferocious fussing of her daughter, whose small leg had caught benumbingly in the wrap.

Presently, Jolene believed she must have fallen into a maze of sorts, as she returned reluctantly over and again to a certain recognizable decline off a certain recognizable path with a deep bend and a pile of unusually stacked rocks, witnessed, all the while, by the gaze of wild beasts.

Determined beyond her natural abilities, Jolene hacked at the bush with her handaxe and in time stumbled forth into the clearing that would one day hold Acacia.

A bird descended from the sky. Elysium. The vulture. Landing with its back to the trespassers, it paused and then hopped forward into the clearing, extending its wings as it capered along. Jolene followed.

And it was there that she received instant knowing.

For asudden before her, Jolene discerned a house—a specific house—where none was yet built. Stately, a refuge, set-apart, the grand residence was enveloped in a kind of aether; a supernal substance, porous and misty, but substantive enough to accommodate the body and its exploration.

Reaching this vision, the vulture loped past her up the porch stairs, then toured Jolene and Salome across the threshold, and through the foyer, and into the great room, and then up the interior staircase, and through each room, perfectly appointed, and at each juncture the bird instructed Jolene as to Heaven's charge: that she give flesh to its incorporeal state.

Mrs. Jolene Nightingale did not return that day with the root that harrowed her. No, it was a holy woman and daughter who came down from the mountaintop, burning no longer with feverish desire, but with revelation.

And this renewal of purpose served her well, for not long after these events her husband, the sole proprietor of Nightingale Lumber, perished.

❦ The Death of The Patriarch

The specific circumstances were these—one Tuesday midnight, the husband of Jolene Nightingale pored over the ledger books of his company in a field tent with cot and coffee kettle, newspapers, and a half-empty bottle of Tennessee whiskey.

Outside the tent stood a significant tree—a Methuselah of the forest—with a rigid-barked trunk so thick the link of two grown men's arms could not encompass it. Though slated for clearing the following day, the ledgers clearly show that this magnificent tree had not yet been delimbed of its lower branches, nor had it been notched, nor had it felt the bite of a crosscut saw. And yet still, in the grave of night, it gave of its integrity and toppled across the patriarch's tent.

The husband of Jolene Nightingale was a sturdy man. Though his leg, arm, and a portion of his chest were crushed-in, he very well might have lived had his subordinates set to work in haste dissembling the great tree.

For yea, three dozen seasoned lumberjacks lay within eye- and earshot. But the men slumbered-on, lapsed under a dullness like death, and not a one heard the dire crashing, nor the proprietor's lamentations. Past the pre-dawn commencement of the workday, the workers dreamt instead of the building of a spectral kingdom, a communal nightmare shared presently, upon waking past noon, as the men ardently hacked together the fallen limbs covering their captain.

When the men had finally cut through the tree, several took to inspecting it. There they found no sign of blight nor cause of collapse—no hollowed trunk, proliferated with the small tunnels of borer beetles that sometimes carve out the innard flesh while the exterior bark still presents as sound. No, the tree was whole—by all avid judgments, thriving. And beneath that mass of branch and leaf, the men found their perished captain, fixed with a visage of deep consternation.

Jolene Nightingale embraced her widowhood as due inheritance and with apparent dignity—with hard, long swallows, dabbed eyes, dowdy mourning clothes, and dire memorial luncheons for Mr. Nightingale's grieving associates. In truth, though, her soul was tranquil, for she had already received secret knowledge and turned toward more Heavenly pursuits.

After her requisite social obligations, she finalized the settling of her husband's estate. Her harvest was a considerable fortune of property promptly sold, thriving accounts cashed-in, and equity in his business bought out by silent parties back east. And yea, having achieved such wealth, Jolene could have returned home and lived the luxurious society life she had so recently pined for. But no, she withdrew, departing quickly from the expectations of widows, and turned secretly to her charge from winged Heaven.

And so began the veiled construction of the Pear House, named for the color of the luxuriant root Jolene had so desired when early with child. To dissuade any attention garnered by her deceased husband's stature, Jolene Nightingale enlisted the help of suppliers and distant laborers with no connection to the region. Conscripting their efforts at rates far superior to her late-husband's, and thereby also securing their discretion, Jolene imported materials with strict orders that all be hauled into the thicket under the cover of night, guided solely by herself and illuminated by her single, slender candle protected by a glass vase, determining that a slower pace in construction would return its value in future seclusion.

Jolene knew she was to build the Pear House to those certain specifications she had received from the vulture; knew the wood ought be culled from the durable acacia tree, which grew sporadically in the thicket amongst the thriving regional pines; knew that, tended well, the estate would span an epoch. The shape of the Pear House would be a rectangle, which ascended two floors and extended as long as six frontier log houses, with a lone central staircase. The ground floor would be entirely open with a large kitchen on the eastern flank. The upper floor, however, would harbor many small rooms, built so that each connected to the others with doors on either side, and built with double-hung windows to bless the Pear House with every relieving thicket breeze. And finally, there were to be two primary suites: Jolene's, in the back, eastern corner, facing the woods, and her daughter, Salome's, similarly designed, but occupying the front, western wall, so that the growing child would have the benefit of Acacia's peculiarly mirrored sunrise.

As always, Jolene Nightingale cared much for ornamentation. Though Heaven's task was to erect the building's fundamental stature, her secondary nature took to importing lavish furniture from estate sales in the northeast to make the Pear House a place of marvelous beauty. No sum was spared toward her Edwardian cabinetry and armoires, dignified French tables, grand Kilim woven rugs, gilded mirrors, Fabergé trinkets, and accordion writing desks for each room.

Still, in exceptional time, the Pear House was completed. The workers' final silence was ensured with a hefty addendum to their wage as Jolene Nightingale escorted the workers back through her maze of the thicket one last time. Not a one of them would ever set foot in Acacia again.

❧ A Hermitage No Longer

Now, all Jolene wished for was independent widowhood, and above all, isolation. To bounce Salome, her high-spirited daughter, on the knee, to sing her down for naps, to walk the thicket upending roots, to drive her blue pickup when the fancy struck her to some nearby town for a sugar stick. And this privacy she achieved for a measure of time. But Heaven did not see fit for them to remain solitaire.

Yea, through the dark thicket, a fisherman from Galveston arrived. Next, a vagabond with his cloth bindle. Soon, a convict, escaped from his confinement in the Sugar House Prison of Utah. From pasts soon forgotten, there arrived more widows. And more runaways, as I was, we seekers of a new dawn. Jolene Nightingale did not know whether to let them remain or to send them away, but communing with the vulture's knowing eyes, settled at last upon the idea that as she had been given this place in her time of need, so too would it be for those Heaven shepherded to her city of refuge. And so it was that, possessed of the remains of her family fortune and having built the Pear House to seemingly accommodate them, Jolene Nightingale found herself the matriarch of an empyrean hall.

As for the dozen-odd travelers, they found asylum in the abundance of small rooms furnished beyond their wildest luxuriations. Some even believed these were designed to fulfill their deepest inner wishes, as though Jolene and the dwelling had foreknown their coming.

For a time, Jolene Nightingale abided the passivity of her guests. But soon the liability of their unoccupied minds and bodies grew apparent. She thereby provisioned them with necessary activities: the tilling of a splendid garden; the summons to calisthenics in the yard; the construction and tending-to of chicken coops and pigsties; and their morning and evening devotionals — offering them gems of wisdom afforded to her by visits from the bird — which she read to her flock in the Great Room downstairs.

And after a time, when the arrival of the pilgrims plateaued at twenty, and Jolene's ambitions for the Pear House recessed their intensity, her thoughts turned inward, perhaps for the last time, toward the evidence of her husband's demise. For though she felt no dispiritedness, their union having slowly deteriorated from the very moment of their vows, she was deeply perplexed by the anomaly of the great felled tree.

❧ THE TREE

A kept newspaper contained an article and a black-and-white photograph of the severed behemoth. Nagging suspicions played on Jolene's mind like feral shadows. As she read and reread the newspaper's account, Jolene knew the tree as her co-conspirator; an accomplice. Often, even in the bright of day when occupied by some task, she felt she was sitting amongst its branches, perhaps leaning the weight of her great soul against its upper reaches. She became convinced, in time, she'd aided and abetted its fall.

These ruminations produced a new obsession—she would certify the solvency of the ample trees encircling the Pear House, lest the spirit of her husband topple one on her in turn.

Among *the saints*—an endearment Jolene gave to those souls who had arrived first to Acacia—was one Matthew Paxton, heralding from the great Pacific Northwest. As for his prior occupation, Paxton claimed he'd conducted fish, wildlife, and forestry excursions for the region's numerous national parks. Deputized by Jolene, Paxton secured a number of specific tools, purchased by the estate's coffers. With these he drilled into each nearby tree to ensure its solidity, and conducted examinations of the foliage to check for the presence of hostile insects. Likewise, along with these specific supplies, which Jolene and Matthew secured via a post office in the not-too-distant town of Clementine, arrived the mis-shipment of several crates from New Jersey containing prototypes for a new kind of rake, heavy iron and readily capable of hacking away brush and bramble with its thick conal spikes.

Paxton's findings as he scrutinized the trees: nothing. The trees were sound, the bugs, non-burrowing. But rather than assuaging her fears, this disappointed Jolene Nightingale, for she had determined to ease her soul by reference to some deficiency of the woods. Paxton was competent, but not omniscient, in truth, no expert, and time would soon show the dual nature of his soul. But before he was relieved of this surveying task, he made another request—that Jolene secure a book he was familiar with to expand his current scrutiny.

Jolene improved upon his request by ordering this book and more, undertaking the purchase of a very particular library brimming with books on nature and agriculture. And these, supplemented with selections of a spiritual quality, her new-found passion. Surrounded by such a wealth of knowledge, Jolene thereby permitted her saints to a reasonable amount of time for study, guiding by point and counterpoint in the shaping of Acacia's revelatory theology.

But the presence of spiritual books, containing stories of the beginning and the beyond, of holy forest beasts, of age-old mysteries, of vengeful serpents and profane specters, only enhanced her troubles. For as Paxton's evaluations failed to cause her fears to wane, Jolene Nightingale began to hear — from a certain place in her bedroom, from the woodcut statue of a bird that sat on her nightstand — a voice.

It whispered short snatches of knowledge only two souls could possibly know — personal lore, like the place of their first coupling in Nashville; and his pet name for her, Jolly, from early on in their courtship; and her embarrassment at her singing voice. Jolene knew it was her husband from somewhere in the aether who had returned to issue these susurrations. Showing his hand, the malevolent spirit of her husband abused her; tried to break her. She had lent her unreined spirit to the fated tree, unseated it from the earth, and when the bulk toppled over, disavowed him so cavalierly. His spirit promised Jolene a full measure of ruin.

Yet throughout these torments, a slip of her husband's tongue produced a flicker of renewed confidence. Unwittingly, he affirmed the beauty of the Pear House. For who wouldn't admire such a place? Even the Devil himself. Her husband intimated she had built a sanctuary for the hunted; a place of celestial security; a city of jubilee. Should she maintain her presence within the walls of this sacred structure, she reasoned, perhaps he could do her no harm.

The saints of the Pear House rallied behind their Jolene Nightingale as she refused to leave her domain. Understanding theirs was a patronship unable to ever be repaid — such bounty of food, shelter, camaraderie, seclusion, ornamentation, and spiritual enrichment — some took on cooking for the group; others went for supplies when she bade them with distinct instructions each trip; others delegated themselves as gardeners. And some concerned themselves with the care of Salome, a girl now of six, especially Matthew Paxton, who asserted himself with eagerness before Jolene thought to demote him for his recent failures of aptitude.

Thus, one foggy morning, during Salome's tutored rounds with Matthew Paxton, the two peering over a patch of green roots which had sprouted at the edge of the thicket, Paxton thumbed the botany tome he had taken to carrying, muttering all the while. While his attentions scanned pictures and indexes and phylum charts to identify this peculiar specimen, Salome removed her pocketknife, severed a little portion, and rushed the brûlée to her mouth.

Like her mother Jolene before her, Heaven's talon reached down and tore away her veil. Salome likewise then received her second sight and discerned a series of chimeric visitations:

First, she beheld the spirit of her father, hovering above them in the trees, haranguing her with insults. Next, lithe hypnotic women, blurred at their edges, sashayed through the brambles, fleeing inward just as she sighted them. After which, Salome espied not her single shadow as one sees naturally emanating from themselves, but in the rippling of light through the leaves above, three, each distinct in form, manner, and clothing.

The smallest shade, true to her present form, climbed a nearby tree. A second in a wide and flowing garment stood still and upright. And finally, a third, hunched over with grey hair, hobbled around her in a circle.

And again, beneath these forms, Salome's gaze penetrated the earth as though the soil was a surface of glass. There, she perceived tremendous caverns roofed by stalactites, and in that abyss, legions of glowworms that spun incandescent loops of syrupy beadwork to capture their prey.

And too, as though a newly lit lamp flooded her comprehension, Salome authenticated a series of new structures in the clearing of Acacia. Opposite the thriving garden, across the way from the Pear House, there now rose in her vision a chapel for a new kind of worship she could not yet comprehend. And finally, surrounding the perimeter, spaced out evenly like the numbers of a clock, stood a series of twelve small wooden sheds, each with a vulture settled upon its rooftop.

In that instant, blessed by vision and consecrated by the messengers of the Heaven, Salome Nightingale, yet a girl of eight, became the Seer of Acacia and the heavy mantel of Heaven shifted onto her tiny shoulders.

For meanwhile in the Pear House, unyielding terror had rendered Jolene Nightingale to her bedroom. She had not ventured out in weeks. Salome was the sole person permitted inside her room, and this requiring a certain practiced knock, peculiarly slow and unobtrusive, and the assent of the voice inside — so faint none could comprehend it save her daughter.

Each day, over long hours of these visits to her mother, Salome exited to the expectant saints of Acacia, waiting downstairs around their long table.

The day is promising, they'd say. What would your mother bid us do? What row needs healing? What supplies need to be fetched — so she is aware, only a single bottle of Heinz remains. Which texts need to be studied?

In addition to her daily orders for the saints, Salome also relayed instructions for building the new structures she had seen in her visions.

☙ THE BUILDING OF ACACIA

Construction began in haste. And the saints' labor, in full, was realized: First, the twelve sheds. Each with its purpose, each fashioned of sturdy wood and a padlocked door, each built proportionally spaced from the others so that the clearing between would still appear pleasing.

Next, before the Pear House stretched a greatly improved garden, now planted with okra, chard, squash, tomatoes, and root crops to satisfy an expected swell in their ranks.

Immediately opposing the living quarters, across the span of a quarter-acre on the other side of the garden, lay the completed chapel — constructed just as it was revealed to young Salome Nightingale — a modest one-story structure, narrow but exceptionally long. On the front of the chapel, a small, outcropped foyer with a thick wooden door supported an elegant, rounded steeple outfitted with muted-green overlapping shingles, like the scaly belly of a wyvern. Along the perimeter of the roof, Heaven had dictated a waist-high fence, like a widow's walk, or even a rooftop patio, perfect for a lovely cocktail hour as the sun set in the east of Acacia's thicket, had this building not been designed for ceremony.

For inside, through the small foyer's double doors, Acacia's principal area for worship awaited. With its dais occupying the back, the entire open interior was finished with whitewashed shiplap boarding, giving the chapel the look of a sleek, landlocked boat.

And lastly, heralding back to that winged path-breaker who had revealed Acacia and the Pear House to her mother Jolene, Salome guided the people to craft the likeness of the vulture from the stump of the great tree that had crushed her father, for this effigy would bless their house of worship and before it they would pray.

How the saints of Acacia did revisit that fabled stump in the still of many nights, how they uprooted it, and hauled it back with chain lanyards through the brush. In the garden, how they sculpted the stump with axe and chisel as Salome stood guard over their labor like a small mystical fox.

Now faced by hand-hewn benches that could comfortably sit three saints side by side, a narrow central aisle led to the dais at the back of the chapel. There, the saints placed the effigy of the vulture, that it might brood over their worship, receive their pleas, and intercede for them with Heaven.

Yet in all, it was a noble province, set under wholesome trees, provisioned by Divine favor, and quarantined by Heaven's formidable barrier—the inhospitable bramble, thorn and swamp, serpents, fire ants, alligators, boars, and the disownment of county boundaries.

❧ MAN'S SEDITION AND HEAVEN'S APPOINTED SUCCESSOR

But the June air wore Acacia as a dark, woolen cloak. For still, Matthew Paxton held his rake across his knees. He was thoroughly grimed from a sweltering day's labor in the garden, but a devouring fervor in his grey eyes belied all exhaustion. He presided over some four other men with rakes, who sat around him well past Salome's summons for supper.

And still, when dinner was completed and the dishes washed and restacked, and the children had scurried to their bookshelf for an evening story, nine-year-old Salome led a group of women bearing candles from the Pear House toward the chapel. Suddenly adjusting the symmetry of their walk, she steered her attendants through Paxton's hushed circle, then stopped to pluck a carrot from his basket and bit into it, dirt and all. As she chewed, all the while holding Paxton's grey eyes, her spittle turned to mud, which she swallowed with apparent satisfaction, as if it were a chunk of caramel from a candied apple.

When Salome and the women departed, Paxton's men confirmed his suspicions in mistrustful tones — and was it not also so: that though the girl had walked through their freshly upturned garden earth, she left no footprints? What phantasm touched the earth and yet touched it not? What specter?

Another planting season arrived. As had become customary, Salome entered her mother's room (after that peculiar knock of hers) to receive the order for seeds, clothing, household wares, candy bars for the children, and creature comforts for her mother. These Salome recorded in a ledger, afterwards placing the estimated funds and hand-drawn maps in leather billfolds to deliver to the saints, who would set about procuring the list in small and divided numbers from hardware and dry goods stores across the nearby counties.

But on this morning, as Salome left her mother's room with orders to the Acacians worshiping in the chapel, she again encountered Paxton and his lesser men, who huddled together in rooms further down the hall like a shadowy nativity. This time, as Salome passed, they leapt forward and seized the girl of ten, gagged and bound her, and under the cover of their fellow saints deep in worship in the chapel, deposited her in a nearby shed.

Returning to the Pear House, Paxton and his men entered Jolene Nightingale's bedroom for the first time. Their aim was singular: to separate Acacia from its riches.

But inside that room, with the candles flickering low and the velvet curtains drawn and the ashtray sparkling clean, it was not a dismayed Jolene Nightingale they met, protesting their infiltration of her chambers, nor was it the anticipated coffers of Acacia, glittering with fortune like a slain corsair's grotto.

Instead, the intruders found a grand brass bed with its decorative posts draped in stately semi-sheer heirloom lace. In place of its blankets, neatly drawn, someone had planted a bedding of richly tilled soil nine-inches thick atop the bare white mattress. Thriving ryegrass and a plenty of colorful wildflowers there sprouted. Bees tended blooming azalea. Worms thrived in the mulch. Bright pink pampas fluttered in the breeze of an oscillating fan at the corner of the room.

And atop this inner garden, the decayed corpse of Jolene Nightingale rested, as if on a pyre.

A striped Orb Weaver spun a web from her nosebone to the radial knob of her wrist. A family of Hercules beetles probed the exposed metatarsals of her feet. A thick red-headed centipede draped the entirety of one of her ribs like the detached strap of a loose corset.

Dismayed and disgusted, Paxton and his men commenced their vandalism, stripping drawers from the armoire, scattering Jolene's nightclothes, and turning out her closet, even staving in the fine auburn closure of the accordion desk. Therein, they found the only thing of material value: a cedar cigar box containing several thousand dollars.

This small fortune apparently satiated the insurgents, for before the remainder of the Pear House grew suspicious, these men with rakes fled into the thicket.

There, the mutineers met their just deserts — some on the piercing tusks and stumped teeth of hungered wild boars — others from an agonizing descent into the dark underreaches of the swamp — but Matthew Paxton, separated from his lessers, and carrying the bounty, endured the perplexing convolutions of the bramble and a buffet of the thicket's many torments before succumbing to madness and dehydration, a water moccasin clamped firmly to his inner thigh as Heaven's barrier swallowed the sounds of his delirium.

When their worship was exhausted, the chapel let out and the Acacians returned to the Pear House. There they discovered the ajar bedroom door, so routinely sealed, and the ransacked room of Jolene Nightingale, and her bedded corpse. Dejection swallowed them. For despite such abomination: Where was Salome, their beloved child? A search commenced. And soon she was found, stored in the nearest shed. She had rolled to the corner, stripped the gag from her mouth on a break of wood, and huddled herself among the field mice, who'd woven themselves around her like a surging carpet. Recovered, yes, but for a time still absent, for Salome again communed with Heaven.

The saints were benumbed. No eldership had been established; no candidate was capable of ascension. Theirs was a community dependent on a figurehead, and any with such ambition had already succumbed to the scheme of Matthew Paxton, the first seditionist of Acacia.

Testimonies vary. Some say a year. Some a day. But in her own time, the Prophetess Salome Nightingale returned from the city in the clouds; back to her body; to that bedroom; to that room I came to know as preserved for ceremony. Not a single voice raised dissent. Her mother gone, it was young Salome Nightingale, imbued fully with favor, who would lead Acacia into dark or dawn.

And so, there in the now-agéd Nightingale's garden, with this expanse of arcana laid bare before us, I, Petra, pulled back my lips, as she did hers, to let my teeth elongate. I plucked, as she did first, nibbling the thin meat of the mouse's haunch. Our beaks, they touched. Intimately we fed.

Returning to the Pear House, I saw the Nightingale to her room. I drew her bath and bathed and dressed her, then triple-plaited her hair while she smoked her pipe and studied the operating manuals of the Maytag washer and dryer Acacia had just acquired at the Black Friday sale in the nearby town of Clementine.

Though the hour had gone late, the Mother suggested on a whim that we might visit the machines right then, set up downstairs in the corner of Fleur's kitchen. We might run a load too, and admire the spin cycle, and the efficient engineering of its modest decibel level, and best of all, the sudden whoosh at the start when the basin fills with water. That sound tingled her netherparts, the Mother confessed with a kittenish simper, the same way as soaring on the Rapture.

The Rapture—I must take this moment to chronicle the Nightingale's love for Acacia's rope swing, set high in the branches of the grandest oak in our clearing, next to the chapel.

When good humors found the Nightingale, she climbed the tall tree and wrapped her legs around the Rapture's bench seat, fashioned from a small piece of 2x4. Taking a strong grip on the thick knots tied into the rope, she'd scoot off the branch, whooping as she plummeted, then rose again, then fell, then rose a little less, while all the saints below cheered.

It was an endearing vision of the Nightingale — thirty seconds of her sailing hair and panting smiles and eyerolls and ripples of giggling screams. Thirty seconds when the Prophetess rejected haruspex, and in this moment as close to flying as a bird worshipper can get, found herself roiling with two stripes of ecstasy.

Oh, never mind the appliances, she suggested. Let's visit the Rapture. There is a blood moon rising.

My heart quickened. My mother and I had spent many warm and tender evenings on my swingset at the Jesper farmhouse, flushing wide our bare toes in the humid air. This before I hung myself with the quiver and she ordered the swingset sold for scrap.

I waited while the Prophetess trimmed her candles and covered the bird cages, and she did then loan me one of her thick woolen cloaks with the large hoods. Though I can't say for certain why, we neglected the hallways and the doors and climbed out the window, landing clumsily and with giggles, though we did not draw a wink of attention. We began our walk across the grounds.

Before us loomed the new place of worship—the orb—or the frame of it anyway, only a few of the panels yet affixed, and these glinting in the moon's shine. I thought it looked like a sci-fi spaceship, and I said so. Or perhaps like a golf ball that Heaven had chipped from the sand pits of the stars and sunk half into the ground. The Nightingale looped her arm through mine and gave my observations the benefit of her strange chirping laughter, pitched far too high for her sonorous speaking voice.

Though we'd planned to swing, she steered me toward the orb. When we reached the crossbeams, she unlinked our arms and ducked underneath. I followed her in there, into that disquieting place, and in doing so felt that I had transgressed into the ribcage of some ancient creature, some Leviathan decomposing on the earth, the sky disrupted by the lattice of its bones.

The Nightingale toured me around each of its principal supports, knocking her knuckles against the wood as though to assure herself they were solid. She picked up a small piece of construction chalk and began to draw little stick figures on the wood—a girl laying down, a bird, the rain, some flowers. Although we went slowly, beam to beam, I grew dizzy, a sense of dread overcoming me even as I wished to draw within the orb's majesty and comprehend it in full. I stumbled into the soft dirt of Acacia as she lauded the structure, and my palm closed around an object there in the grass. As I turned over and looked up, the Nightingale stood directly above me, backlit by the moon, and in that still night, her garments did not swirl but lay on her body rigid as the walnut wood of a coffin.

Her close proximity meant I had to back away on my bottom to stand. As I scooted off, I took a glance at the object in my hand. It was a perfect match for the totem I'd found in the body of the fox upon my arrival to Acacia—the gold key ring, embossed with "E. Muir." I began to stammer at the curious relic, but the Nightingale bent forward and squared me by the shoulders and slapped me across the face. I quieted, ashamed, and she did not comfort me. Yea, she did not speak at all in our solemn procession back to the Pear House, the Rapture too special a gluttony for this spoilt evening.

I saw her to her room, where she again affected a measure of kindness and invited me to climb into her bed and watch television. But citing my weariness, I left her with a firm kiss on the back of the head, just above the floral sterling barrette securing her braid for slumber.

I did not return to my room as I'd intimated I would. I visited the Son in his room the next door over. He was sitting upright in his bed, glasses balanced crookedly across the jutted bone of his boyhood broken nose. Likable, loveable, I threw his book aside, for what interest does *The History of Western Philosophy* carry against a Prophetess's castle?

I made him swear up and down, port to starboard, the book on the floor, spine split on Baruch Spinoza, and all the Pear House knew our pleasure.

Dear Vigilant Reader,

With one hand the Nightingale maimed, refreshing with the other. A bone fist and a velvet glove.

On the night Heaven freed me from such protracted kinship with the Nightingale and sent me on its deadly errand of judgment to her bedroom — perhaps postponing such lethal intervention only until after I had received from her my legacy, our heritage — I experienced a shocking and profound displacement of mind. For this reason, I did not write in my little books in my usual manner, nor for several nights afterwards. But there is continuity in the account, for celestial wisdom impressed itself upon the Nightingale's Son and he recorded the events that transpired while I lay in my trance. Readily, I introduce the Son's writing into this account, so the reader may have the authentic narrative of the Nightingale's passing and the final ascent of me, Petra, the Prophetess of Acacia.

From the writings of the Son:

> After we had prayed, Petra Caldwell went forth alone from the place where her saints of Acacia had met in the thicket. Inching forward on her belly, she reached the steps of the Pear House, then crawled over the threshold and ascended the staircase, pausing at the end of the great hallway, training her ear toward the room at the end, that of the Prophetess Mother Salome Nightingale. Petra then transgressed the hallway with the soundless ease of the serpent, though confident and secure, having already redeemed the allegiance of this author along with the men with rakes nearby the Mother's room.
>
> In that grandest place in the Pear House, in the room of the Mother, the birds slept soundly in cages draped with thick counterpanes, for here arrived a night requiring their silence. In her right hand, Petra carried her rake, half-chopped of its stock to achieve an ease of swing within the Mother's room.

Petra then opened the door and crossed the threshold. Extinguishing the velvet bedside lamp and candles so only the moon illumined that space, Petra's sight found no hindrance as Heaven provided her the clarity of its judgment. The Mother lay in her bed, her eyes closed, arms outstretched, deep in slumber.

Petra then leapt upon her, striking the base of the Nightingale's throat with her rake, driving its spines into her neck, then again into her chest. Though the Nightingale bled heavily, Petra stood over her and again delivered her rake. A third time, again. This assured Heaven's will was done.

Petra then did lay waste to every painted likeness of the Prophetess in that bedroom and likewise in our hallway, afterwards shucking the dressers and armoires of their ceremonial clothing and rending them to shreds, afterwards throwing the Nightingale's many written accounts out the windows and into the garden. And finally, after all afterwards, when her fervor had subsided, Petra made her way outside where the saints of Acacia, those already loyal and those quickly becoming so, had assembled. There, she bade they should amass all the Nightingale's wreckage into a pyre.

And when this was done, Petra charged it should be lit. Derobing herself, Petra danced. And in the presence of Acacia, she assumed her rightful place, calling out that the age of the Nightingale had passed and that she, Petra Caldwell, had received the mantel of Heaven and was the true Prophetess of Acacia.

Some claimed that night that they glimpsed Petra ascend into Heaven. Some claimed it was in a fiery chariot, and that she gravitated the stars behind her like a meteor shower, reversed from its natural plummet and escalating instead into the spheres. Others said it was within the eye of a tempest, one with winds so ethereal they passed through the fibers of Acacia and did not extinguish a single candle. Others claimed she morphed into a giant bird and took flight to fortify the thicket against the coming Commotions.

Claims aside, when morning came and Acacia rose to a new epoch of worship, all saints found with certainty that the body of the Nightingale was gone and that Petra slept alone atop the bed in her room.

The Son's remarks concluded, I present now *my* reflections on forgiveness and the judgment of the Son for his long role in my sufferings as recorded in my little books.

BOOK XI

TO ERADICATE ANIMUS
& THE JUDGMENT of the SON

Not to haphazardly absolve. Not to offer trite lenience. Not to whipstitch the wound when only sutures will seal the gash. These gestures soothe but must by definition retain the legacy of offense. True absolution means to excavate.

To carry out such expunction, one must first transgress time. Travel to the sites of greatest grievance, and there delve a well. To penetrate the undercurrents below, one must chart a map of each dramatis, its characters, and their workings with a cartographer's precision.

Then one must proceed into the caverns of their wounding as does the relic hunter in order to discover the site of utmost consequence — the *locus terriblis* — where fingerlings bloom in the soul's furtive terrain. There, the relic hunter must pummel with potent tools — Heaven's power, so much greater than themselves — to excise the offending blight.

Not to recklessly forgive. Instead, one must delimb the savored wound.

As for the Son of the Nightingale, himself a glowering seedling sprouting at a crossroads: Who more than he had so perversely

both adored and disfigured me, performing his Mother's cruel-
ties, while our lips met and his tongue lapped across my teeth?

All of Acacia crowded into the chapel to witness how I'd work
out his conviction. The air outside had turned a waxy gray. No
one thought of their labor, or the Rapture, or the Commotions,
or their empty stomachs grumbling for lunch, or sack races, or
whether I'd lost all reason — my nude dance around the fire, my
Heaven-sanctioned peepshow, just one-night past.

At the head of our assembly, I stood in a laborer's tunic. I held
my scepter — my rake — still crimson from its earlier work in the
Nightingale's bedroom.

And at my feet, the Son bent down and willingly stretched his
head across the altar, exposing his handsome neck.

I heard nothing. Felt nothing. At that moment, not his quiet
anguish, nor the saints and their expectations. I was singularly
attuned to what lay beyond the window of the chapel, dotting
the perimeter of Acacia.

My sheds.

Of the array of options Heaven fanned before me like a deck of slickback playing cards, I could deal the Son my blow — or deal him pardon — or imprison him in my choice of these, my sheds — storm his doors at my fancy — starve him — watch him devolve to skin-wrapped bones — or feed him my feast — then release him under the moon only to track him in the thicket — and haul him babbling back — or sing him my sweet song — hold and kiss his head and wipe the blood and pus from his face — or smuggle him his own set of little books and pens and mount him covenants of my love, in our lake, in the truck, in his bed, in our dirt — and whisper him promises of a future.

Dear Merciful Reader,

Somewhere in my stomach, I made allowance for the Son. Part beneficence, part advantage, part foreknowing, for I knew an even greater threat festered. Even from the grave, the Nightingale had a hidden card in the muslin of her death shroud. Years before, she'd pulled it, slapped it on the table, and took every bet made.

Her prodigy—the promised Boy.

With a mother's cunning, she had fashioned Acacia a pretender— home grown, adored by all—from Fleur's pregnancy; an account of which I intend to share with you in due time if I may plead your patience a few pages longer. Although but a child of seven at the time she was deposed, he at once carried the dual shades of a dark, vengeful angel and a merciful, shielding wing in the Commotions to come. Raw meat to trap prowling wolves, the Boy was a diversion to lengthen the Nightingale's tenure, and her beguilements had lodged and reshaped the theology of Acacia. As long as the Boy remained, the Mother remained too.

I include now a portion of my sparse writings in the intervening years after I had risen to my appointed role of Prophetess. I implore the reader to interpret my words with an awareness of the distress in which they were composed, for I had only recently freed Acacia from the Nightingale's tyranny. Despite this jubilation, I proceeded under the realized weight of my calling, and thusly, with trembling.

BOOK XII

THE MATRICES of LOSS

I am within the matrices. Be gone from me cataclysm!

The true tormenter is removed; years of her anguishments suddenly halted. And yet, I find I am bereft. Longing troubles my rock heart, so defined am I by her legacy. How I wish I could conjure her afresh, brush and bind her brittle hair. Feed her bones with the stories of my father. Cackle with her again at an evening program, shoulder to shoulder in her bed, sharing a bag of our favorite Doritos, passing her pipe back and forth, puffing sweet-cherry smoke rings among the bird cages of her bedroom. Swing the Rapture. And still, again at the end of each night, fingers dusted orange, and crumbs lodged in my teeth, leap to stove in her skull again, and again, and again.

Gratefully, motherhood demands much of me. Tending our flock provides some wanted distraction, and I can reflect on (if not good, at least meaningful) years in the rearview mirror of this Heavenly charge.

Acacia is small, shy a hundred souls, mostly men (and these aging) who soon will prove useless for difficult labor. Our women approach middle age too, circling with their candles in worship, maintaining our ceremonies to forestall the Commotions. Our children seem the site of the most promise, having grown in an age outside her corruption. Once, I dreamt of them marching from Acacia's thicket behind me, still in their jammies, each carrying a cut-off rake, and singing our hymns — a Children's Crusade, fed from my breast on undiluted Heaven. I led this marvel on a chariot drawn by birds. Surely Heaven would rearrange the thicket, straighten its curvatures, cure its labyrinth, and let us finally free.

The past auguries of the Nightingale and my own often diverge concerning the security of Acacia. Where the Nightingale fore-told Fleur's Boy as a citadel in the Commotions, my assessment recognizes something uncanny, but renders him differently, in part, because the Boy shows no obvious care for his person or any awareness of his proposed stature or any indication of spiritual affinity. As I've warily watched him grow, I find he wanders constantly into the thicket alone. He sits for long hours in the dirt in the garden, prodding the inners of his soft thighs with the spike side of his rake. One evening after ceremony, I found him on the roof of the chapel, wallowing on his back among the butchered pig meat we'd left there as an offering, cavalier to the pluck of vultures ever nearing his living flesh. When I called him down the ladder, he leapt from the roof while flapping his arms. A portent — or a joke — though I took no pleasure either way.

In some guises, he is phosphorescent, a golden glow surrounding him like a painting of a martyr. But then the hymn known so well to all Acacian saints returns to my lips — *we're after the same rainbow's end* — and I watch him uneasily in moments of mundanity, watch him learning to plant, or frozen in freeze tag while the other children swarm around him, or slumbering sweetly in his bed, and I no longer know if the Boy is some kind of guardian or a spreading cancer or another spiritual matter entire. I only know he holds some measure of significance and have believed so since the day of his birth. Ever vigilant, I carry my rake — my scepter, my sword — like a shepherd's crook in case a sheep's veneer reveals a jackal.

Though I have stewarded our saints faithfully for a small number of years, the coming days are uncertain, and I sense the end. The Desert Father Moses had his tablets; John the Revelator, his isle of dirt; and I, Petra Caldwell, these little books.

BOOK XIII

IN the FULLNESS of TIME, a CLEANSING
& THE WAVE of SOUND
& TO SMITE a SACRED EFFIGY
& THE HIDDEN ROOM of the
NIGHTINGALE
& THE MOTHER'S INTENT for ME
& THE WAKE of GOLDEN PURIFIERS
& A SUSPICION of FOES
& THE SHORN BEAK
& THE DEFIANCE of the BOY
& THE RAMPANCY of MY RAKE
& THE DEVOTION of the SAINTS
& AUGURY and DREAMCRAFT
& FLEUR'S MAULING
& THE POWER of MY EASEMENTS
(& an Interjecting Entry . . .)

If Acacia was to flourish, we required genesis, *tabula rasa*, inception. While the Pear House had been cleansed several years prior, I had yet to turn to the innards of our chapel. I knew in time this obscene oversight — I had ravaged the Nightingale's personal effects, but now, with haste, and above all else, I must purge the chapel of the Nightingale's influence and prune her outgrowth to our dogma.

The saints and I set forward on this errand. The tapestries, lush and gaudy macrame, were shorn from the chapel's walls. The benches too, hacked up and hauled off. The books of our spiritual songs were shoved off the shelves and carted out in wheelbarrows. Working inwards in that thin, long room, we faced the Mother's pulpit.

A latent dread — a persistent creep I had so long shooed away like a pesky child — finally descended and would leave me be no longer. The totality of the Nightingale's words — the cacophony of her encouragements, and prophesies, and curses, and cackles from the day I met her until the day I removed her — returned to me in one immense and suffocating wave of language. Blood poured from my nose; from the thin scar across my forehead.

We pressed on, the saints and I, weights against an impregnable sound, until I reached the pulpit, the stump of another tree, four feet tall, sanded at its plateau, and well-lacquered. I spat upon its surface, though our intent was what lay behind it.

Against the back wall stood the statue of the vulture, carved from the hulking tree that had crushed the Nightingale's father. Standing over seven feet tall, the rudely sculpted frame conferred arcane credibility. The peaks of its drawn wings rose well above its menacing, patinaed face, which sulked deep into the middle of its chest and was set with two dauntless black eyes. The only portion made of metal on this idol was a foot-long curving beak with hollow nostrils protruding from its misshapen head.

I drew my shawls tighter and stepped toward it. In the presence of the saints, steadying me as I raised my arms, I dealt the first blow with the sharp edge of my rake, lodging the instrument deep into the bird's cheek. Exhaustion overwhelmed at this single, prophetic blow, and so I abandoned my rake and ordered the men to topple the remainder of the statue and haul it to the yard to be burned. Then, the saints were to sand down the chapel's walls and ceiling. And they must not ignore the baseboards, or any surface in that place touched by the Nightingale's incense.

Meanwhile, I returned outside to smoke the Nightingale's pipe, to recover myself and oversee them from afar, the vigor of my body squeezed out flat like a used packet of ketchup.

The saints' work carried them through the chapel and into a small chamber behind where the statue once stood. It was a room of little consequence, used for storage and overflow items. Decontaminating this room required the saints to remove a weighty antique armoire, which held our candles and devotionals, along with the thick imported rug beneath it.

Angels sing, discovery. The Son of the Nightingale came swiftly from the chapel door, his face a mask of awe and worry. I spent a minute in its ruddy lines, highlighted with the sluice of soil and sweat, and not fully comprehending his urgency. And so rather than explain, he helped me to my feet and hurried me back inside the chapel to examine their findings.

Hidden beneath the rug, just removed, lay a small trap door, two feet by three, fitted with a thick iron ring.

I ordered all but the Son remove themselves and studied the curiosity with him for some moments, appreciating that its hidden nature carried some consequence. He then hefted the trapdoor—which swung up easily and with nary a creak, suggesting this was no forgotten chamber, but one accessed recently and perhaps often. The opening revealed a steep hand-hewn staircase descending to a dewy cellar. As I ventured down, feeling the wall for guidance as there was no railing, the waning evening light diminished entirely. Familiar scents then greeted me—earthy tobacco, ambrox, and leather—the stuff of the Nightingale's bedroom.

From the pocket of my dress, I removed a Bic lighter and lighted a candle I found on the floor.

The hidden space clarified. Ten feet in width and fifty deep, the room ran well underneath the chapel. The walls were unfinished, composed of the red rich clay of the earth, and teeming with worms and tangled roots. No sun nourished this chamber, and yet still, a thick bed of grass and wildflowers grew beneath my feet.

Against the far wall, as if emerging from the teeming flora, the only furnishing loomed: a massive farmhouse table, cluttered with a dozen candles in jars. Lighting these too, I investigated the items scattered across its surface: gallon-sized Ziploc bags of the Nightingale's aromatic cherry tobacco; jugs of moonshine; several open cash boxes bursting their moist bills like buttered meat from lobster tails; and my two confiscated keychain charms from E. Muir (one pocketed upon arriving to Acacia and the other found within the skeletal orb) along with his little inscribed wooden box that held the nails for my shoes. Last of all, a large metal trunk sat grimly beneath the table.

I hauled the trunk up and cleared off space and set it before me. It was green, and dented, and fastened with leather straps, sealed off with a silver padlock. I struck the lock with my rake and sifted through much detritus before turning my attention to a certain roll of oversized yellowed parchment bound with rawhide. I unrolled the vellum across the desk and did then plant my palms on either side to peer in by candlelight, like some demigod scrying the surface of the earth for whom they may devour.

The parchment contained blueprints. Detailed blueprints in blue ink, on razor thin paper, for constructing Acacia's orb. The lines were delicate and precise, with nary the scuff of a pink eraser. Above the elegant geometry of that sphere, the Nightingale had sketched one of our birds in flight. I lifted my palms and the scroll rolled itself back up.

Deeper in the trunk, I found a series of recent notes on Waffle House napkins, held together with a black hair tie carrying a few of her long, stray wisps. The napkins were covered entirely in the Nightingale's blotted scrawl; her script when communing with breakfast sausage; with Heaven.

Her marks, they horrified. Here were lengthy and indulgent fantasies—joyous ruminations—on my imprisonment in her nearly-completed orb. How I'd rave there, the Mother mused, alone in that edifice. She included what rations I'd receive and on what schedule. How my belly would bloat. She planned to watch the slow decay of my clothing, and the thick mats emerging in my hair, and the defining outlines of my bones against draught-tautening skin—for my orbitals would pronounce like warped goalposts, she wrote, and my clavicles present as thin as violin bows. Tyranny in such assured language.

I worship mercy; state of the pure soul. But something attained in me while reading those words. I had missed the Mother's grand fate for me by scarce days—had the orb been completed, and had Heaven not moved my hand, I would have again been the Mother's captive.

I stormed back up the stairs, bidding the Son fetch and deliver this trunk to my room in the Pear House. I would study its contents later. For now I charged back into the thicket. Plundering through the bramble with my rake, I returned to the Mother's private garden where I had buried her body. Like Jolene Nightingale before me, I did then ravage the array of yellow-green jeweled roots that had grown over her hastily planted plot — and I did then, as Salome had to her mother, lay the Nightingale's corpse upon a freshly tilled bed of earth — and I did then afterwards rest beside the despoiled ossein, cartilage, and noxious map-work skin, the creatrix of a necropolitic universe.

Above me, a wake of vultures flickered through the breaks in the soft canopy. They keened such delicacy I had unearthed. I beckoned my golden purifiers land. The first descended, and its wings fanned the breadth of a man's height. It advanced toward the Nightingale's body and me, hopping foot-to-foot, careful, and a touch wobbly, like a child playing hopscotch.

A distorted rasp — a low moan — a shriek — as the bird tested the Nightingale's freshness with the curve of its talon. A beak did then dine on the doomsayer's cheek — and a neck chucked backwards, flushing flesh down the gullet — and others joined to rend the Mother's underarms, and the thin meat of her thighs, her toes, a rip of the ear, a pierce of the mushy eye.

A joy for me, replenishing my birds as they fed. Nibbling with their beaks, as I did mine. I returned to the chapel, deeply satiated, where the saints awaited me. I was giddy, my laughter pouring out like winning slots, and I sat on the ground at the back of room amidst the sawdust and empty water jugs and told blue jokes. But soon, the buoyancy of my cathartic accomplishment in the Nightingale's garden turned to ash in my mouth.

It began with an irk, like the feeling there is an unlocked door when one has left their precious valuables unguarded. I scrawled, swirling designs in the sawdust while I worked out my troubles, and my exuberance, warm like the afterglow of morning lovemaking, wore off entire. What of this wormhole in the back room of the chapel? The truth of it wavered before me like a hypnotist's bauble. And when it clarified, I grew numb, cold.

How could the frail Mother access her hidden room under the heavy armoire? This evidenced loyalty. An intimate, or multiples, but assuredly some persons in confidence beyond the dull saint. It mattered little that they had all pledged me. Some deep allegiance to the Nightingale still festered in Acacia.

At the conclusion of our day's cleansing, the saints returned to our long table in the Pear House where Fleur had prepared us a deserved feast of stream-caught fish, root vegetables simmered with ham hock, and wild berry pie.

Here was their bread. The saints would soon have their circus. For at the head of the table in my grand velvet chair sat the Nightingale's boded Boy. Eight years old, healthy, and well-capable of labor, he appeared placid. Nay, spiritless. While Acacia bore the evidence of our earthly toil, he was shirtless and unsoiled.

And more than the Boy. My attention turned to the second trial in front of him. Primly set between a napkin holder made of bone and a fine sterling set of antique silverware, the smelted metal beak of the chapel's dismembered bird effigy rested upon my plate. It was somber in this tableau, like a shank, a spearhead, the tail of a comet. White china shone through the hole of its nostrils.

Arriving after me in a fatigued but cheery bumble, the saints swiftly found their silence as they grasped the significance of both placements. Doctrine and fealty warbled on the swelling stormwaters of our table.

Within this suspended time Fleur entered from the kitchen carrying a pewter tray with a pyramid of candied yams. Perceiving her child's offense in taking my place, the young woman let her tray drop to the floor and rushed to remove him. This I permitted without acknowledgment, my thoughts flashing back to my father, years before, fortifying the perimeter of our farmhouse after the intruder had disturbed us on the 4th of July . . .

A fence Father digs the ground for, and hutches he erects too, wherein he may shelter to keep watch on the road and nearby treeline. When his labor is done, he sits in the middle of it all and takes stock of his work, like a virtuosic watchmaker: I see his shoulders as they ease, then his straight back as it slumps,

then his head as it rests into the rough mapwork of his palms.
And I kiss his forehead, this ruined man . . .

. . . and I return to the now, and bid the saints of Acacia sit
around my table. Fleur and her aids circle the saints, depositing
their bounty. I stand before my now-empty seat to deliver a
blessing. I draw on the power of that feral vulture's spike
looming before me, and when I speak, it is from the plummeting
of my soul:

—Acacia provisions you. It reveals the hallway of
Heaven. It tends the eternity you feel expanding
in your hearts.

[They look at me with admiration.]

. . . Acacia provides the garments you wear, and
these fish and greens, potatoes and onions, these
berries and cream, and these candied yams from
the imagination of our dear Fleur.
*[I remove myself from the head of the table
and walk around its side, touching
her shoulder with tenderness.]*

. . . Acacia provides your shelter. These walls, this
house, the Pear House . . .

[They nod.]

*[I can imagine a fervent alleluia,
but none yet sounds.]*
. . . delivered to Jolene Nightingale by the bird, with
instructions from Heaven. Acacia provides
your worship, your liturgy, and rites.
[My speech all this while is measured . . .]
. . . Acacia brings our deliverance from the
Commotions, from the end of days, where
blood runs to the bridle and not a life is
precious . . .

[Exultant saints!]

*[and my countenance yet remains calm.
I lay my short-staffed rake across my
shoulder.]*
. . . but as one diseased child spreads the pox, as
one wayward voice disrupts the beauty of

the choir, as one cruel word ruins the bliss of courtship, so do falsifiers blight Acacia.

And with this dire pronouncement, I descended my rake with rampancy amongst our banqueting table. Porcelain plates, pig-flesh, the fish bones, blue and purple berries, cloth napkins, the lace tablecloth, glassware, and splinters of the grand table plumed their viscera like a body squeezed beneath a charger's hoof.

And then I excised the saints from the Pear House. They spilled into the yard like fire ants from a ruined mound, while standing at our doorway, I exhorted their backs with the staff of my rake. From the throne of our porch, I bade them grovel on their bellies, save one muscular younger man. So betrayed, I glared at the saints, while Him, I gripped by the arm as he wept past. Him, I ordered to my chamber, where I pushed Him onto the bed and mounted Him and pursued my due release.

The next morning. I donned a silk kimono and fixed my Folgers in my bedroom. I patted my sojourner on the head as he prayed beside my bed. And then I left the Pear House and found the saints sleeping with the snakes and spiders around the perimeters of the yet-completed orb in the rich barrows of our garden.

The soil was still chilled at the dawning sun, soft and giving between my toes. Stirring the saints awake, I took census like a shepherdess: Trevor, Alice, Mateo, Daniel, Wanda, Esmerelda, the children, the elderly, each and all, nearly a hundred, groggy, yet still penitent. I accounted for all save two. A throbbing abscess, these two. Where was Fleur, and where was her child, the betokened Boy?

A shattered spirit is like melted wax, demolded and grotesque; a spent condom in a movie theatre. Cognizant of its offenses — of the speckled nature of its cancers — the shattered spirit contemplates its fecklessness. The shattered spirit is as good as a hanged child dangling from a swingset. But if contrite, the shattered spirit's death rattle reaches for Heaven. In its cry, Heaven may catch the rank of the soul's breath; it may adjust its wings in the currents, scintillating the morose attrition pouring from its mouth. Heaven will then circle slowly. It will land. Affecting disinterest, it will hop closer, or waddle, then false charge. It will sidle up and pin with its beak and dip talons among the soul's mucus; it will carve out a new form.

Heaven rectifies. A spirit once unbalanced by a light breeze now stands headstrong in the tempest. A spirit that cowered from a rabid bitch that cornered her in a tree ventures boldly into the basilik's cave.

The penitent saints of Acacia, these had been so fashioned. Heaven had tended them well in their night in the garden. They could bar the gates of hell impending. If the Nightingale's promised Boy and Fleur wished to defy me, very well. Their souls would immolate, not mine.

And so I knew warmth huddling in the dirt with my followers, and I saw occasion for fresh affinity with the saints. We sat amidst the garden, crosslegged in a circle. I sent the Son of the Nightingale for bread and milk and entertained the saints' dreams from the night before.

Therein, a series of curious phenomena presented itself. Drawing her lengthy legs beneath her, youthful Mya spoke up in that lolling voice I found so irritating. It seems she'd dreamed of a train, chugging at a steady pace across the empty expanse of the plains. An endless cloudy sky stretched above, which Mya did draw on her previous life as an art student to describe with great beauty as resembling diffusing ink blots in a pail of alcohol.

But the train ran out of track in Mya's dream. Rather than tip and topple at this lack of grounding, Mya said, or even effect a stop, the train continued on across the grassland, perhaps with greater speed. Advantaged by its freedom from the rails, the engine began to wobble, to shift on the loose terrain. The cars behind it likewise pivoted at their couplers. When the entirety of the train had achieved this fomenting momentum, swaying and then rejoining the engine to ripple with its unbound rein, it resembled the motion of a mile-long steel sidewinder.

Looming before the train, at the limit of the plains, a great forest encroached. Close grew closer still, and the train threatened the forest with increased propulsion. Collision grew inevitable. But when the train reached the treeline, it penetrated the border deftly, like a jump rope adept finds nary a challenge in Double Dutch, and with the protraction of its hinges, and with the nimble dodging of its sway, not a single tree in the woods was trampled. An occasional burst of grey chimney smoke blipped above the treeline, Mya said, and the pipe of the train's whistle, like the breath of Heaven, grew so faint as to seem imagined.

As I absorbed this dream, I felt that someone had placed a bag of frozen peas against the small of my back. I myself had had this identical dream once as a girl of seven. I affected a clear countenance for the benefit of the saints, though my thoughts ran as runaway as the spectral train. I recalled how my own dream had been met. I had gone to Father that Sunday morning when I woke and asked if such a thing as a train carrying through the woods was sensible. He was with his fiddle on his chair on the porch of the Caldwell farm, his feet propped-up on a three-legged wooden stool, and he wrenched his little cob pipe out of his mouth and plucked for me a song he made up as he went. The song was about a fool girl named Gully, who tied her shoelaces in knots and traded her dull quarter for three shiny nickels. I cheered until the meaning sunk in, and then I flushed; I must have been red as a cherry Slurpee to find him mocking me.

I had just begun to likewise pronounce Mya's dream cockamamy, taking full delight in the fall of her face, when there arose a shrill wailing behind me, deep within the reaches of the shadowy thicket. The sound rose again and again, like a funereal dirge performed by spirits, and it robbed me of the saints' devotion.

I drew the nearby children to me to shelter them under my wing and nodded at the Son to go after this wonder. He departed quickly with several of our boldest men with rakes; a handful of knights errant, hunting the spectral on their Grail quest.

Moments later, they found the missing Boy and Fleur — inert and supine — along with a sight never before seen in Acacia's thicket. Between the Boy and Fleur, a monstrous creature lay dead.

According to the men, it was four-legged and entirely hairless, its wrinkled charcoal skin pooled about its robust musculature. Its limbs were short, and the eyes wide-set, but the girth of its body was long and substantial, and an open snout revealed a plenty of harpoon teeth, drizzled in Fleur's blood.

The men with rakes carried Fleur to the devastated table of the Pear House, sweeping plates and despoiled food to the floor to make her a space. The Boy followed behind them, unharmed and silent. I called for my medicinal herbs, bandages, and a rare can of Coors Banquet to steady my nerves. Crowded by the saints, I removed Fleur's shredded dress and privately marveled at her curious wounding — parallel lacerations, thin as fishline, crossed her body and wide but shallow punctures roughed her thighs and stomach, peculiar for any creature's fang and clawwork.

A time of tending convened, and by late noon, I had stabilized Fleur. The day had already exhausted my valor, and I longed for solitude and a pipe of infinite tobacco with no risk of tongue bite. I took my leave, and hefting my rake, ventured into the thicket to find and study the offending creature.

Mighty carnage had rent a clearing in that bramble. Sloshes of blood dripped off the broken sticks and thorns. The ground was torn to mulched leaves and mud. And there in the middle of it all lay the *lusus naturae*. I knelt and examined the creature's head; peeled back its rubbery charcoal jaws to reveal its great frontal incisors.

I then turned to the curvature of its haunches and the raw pads of its coarse paws. While performing measurements across its skin, I breathed in its abnormally gamey stench — a cloud of sweat and mud, shit, blight, and rot. And there, I settled the creature's nature — it was a bear; a hairless bear. The assailant of Acacia was nothing more than a typical grand denizen of the woods, though allowed by Heaven to persist without fur and thereby test the mettle of the saints. How it came to be deceased without visible wound would stand as a wonder, for a saint then arrived in the thicket behind me, relaying that Fleur had worsened and would not survive the day without my further tending.

To care for her more comfortably, I ordered the saints carry her upstairs to the bedroom opposite of mine; to the Nightingale's childhood bedroom; to that room equipped for ceremony. Therein, I wheeled the barcart of my salves, tinctures, and cure-alls. Like the Nightingale before me, the saints believed my very breath could raise the dead, but I knew no such huffing would stop the flow of Fleur's blood and I set to work renewing her bandages.

All this while, I reflected on my prior states of convalescence in Acacia. I had been dragged from the thicket, bruised, in wild mind, after my foiled escape. I had been ravaged by the worms. Who had tended me in such sufferings? The Son? No. He lacked the capacity for healing. The Nightingale? How could she have lengthened my life when she knew Heaven's plan for us? Did she know? How could she preserve me, the instrument of her ruin?

When at last I determined Fleur would not perish, I returned downstairs and took solace in my velvet chair at the head of our table.

The saints surrounded me, atremble for news. A tea service was set, and I lit the Nightingale's pipe, preparing to manage the saints' tremors. I hid my own angst behind a bravado of slow, deep puffs, returning my unoccupied right hand to my dress's pocket, where all day, during moments of contemplation, I had worried my newly recovered leather charms, discovered within the Mother's subterranean abysm beneath our good saints' honest chapel.

Rather than offer base comfort for my saints, a story seemed opportune, and under the influence of these amulets and such timely events I settled at once on a story of great significance to Acacia. A story I myself had recounted in wonder in an earlier volume of my little books as it concerned me, and our wounded Fleur, and the genesis of the Boy. A story of the wayward angel who appears in so many guises, the *originali dominus* of my charms — Mr. Edgar Muir.

Dear Inquisitive Reader,

I interject into the continuity of this account to graft in this much earlier entry concerning E. Muir, recorded in my little books during the latter days of my solitary confinement.

I interject so that you, dear Reader, might benefit from the story at this opportune moment, as did the saints who lived again this experience through my retelling, and with trembling, revelation, and gasp, curse, and sob. As the beating of a single moth's wings sets off a certain causality — as a candle must burn toward only one end — as even the sun may not hang its golden majesty for eternity — so did the fulfillment of Mr. Muir's dark miracle set Acacia on a celestial course which continues to mystify me to this day.

But in the moment of his arrival, before Mr. Muir's night of terror commenced, we knew him only as another cheerful saint who had been guided into our hamlet — as one more lost lamb welcomed into the folding as the Mother Nightingale stood evening watch with her shepherd's rake:

☙ Mr. Muir

When the man with the sugar sticks emerged from the thicket and onto our grounds, we delighted at a new member of our flock. The man wore a fine cream suit and a faded green baseball cap with a net back. He carried a large, well-worn doctor's satchel with a ribbed alligator-skin handle and walked with a waddle. Beneath his suit jacket, at the waistband, he wore a leather holster, the kind you might spy a dozen times on a day in Texas, though it was empty of those firearms so forbidden in Acacia. News of his arrival set the saints to report, for he had not been guided through the bafflements of the thicket from the eastern side as was typical for the rest of us. No, he had entered from the recently-flooded inlet connected to the Lake O' The Pines in a small rowboat.

The Nightingale sent out the women with candles first and they surrounded him in the garden in their gentle way while she greeted him from the porch. The Nightingale then bade him cross the threshold and enter the Pear House.

The man's name was Mr. Edgar Muir and he hailed from the eastern portion of this country. As for his occupation, he was a litigator; a creature who manipulates speech to affect the judgments of others. Though Mr. Muir told stories of his deplorable profession, he was possessed with a certain delicate charm that set Acacia at ease. Beyond that, he was one who did not present with sweat, despite the heat, and despite his exertion so recently paddling up the inlet.

At Mr. Muir's feet sat his traveling suitcase — the leather doctor's bag. When the Nightingale inquired if he had brought something to Acacia as a gift, Mr. Muir sat forward on the edge of his chair and returned that his bag held treats, for he often kept up his energies with these striped dime-store sugar sticks. Mr. Muir then asked whether some of the small children before him might enjoy a sampling. This was assented. Acacia's children, numbering only twelve at that time, clamored before the bag, and Mr. Muir fielded their queries on the flavors — root beer, watermelon, butterscotch, sour green apple, and so many more — with indulgent joy. The rest of Acacia were then given their own pick — I believe that Kingston selected cotton candy. And a lime for Delilah, for Delilah did love lime.

When all had made their choice and unwrapped their prizes, Mr. Muir leaned back in his chair and crossed his legs in a lengthy pose and laced his stubby hands together over the firm swell of his stomach. The children passed their sugar sticks around, sharing licks, and each face in the Pear House did then resemble something like holiday joy. Except for the Nightingale's. She wore a moody look, at war with our merriment, sulking around, casting her broody eyes, and even refusing Mr. Muir's generous offering for herself.

From somewhere in the room, difficult to pick out from the clamor, the soft, strange hum of a familiar tune emerged. Soon, other saints caught its melody, and when they did, they hushed as I. Stillness began its rule, and at last, I located the source of the sound. It came from Mr. Muir's chair. His lips remained as placid as a ventriloquist's. But when the quiet reached a sufficient threshold, he leaned forward in his chair and broke sweetly into song:

Who can build a palace?
Split it to its core?
Mix up old religions and make up for their wars?

    The Candyman.
    The Candyman can.

Who can cross an ocean?
Sink into the deep?
Name all the behemoths and the company they keep?

    The Candyman.
    The Candyman can.

Mr. Muir's voice was like the soothing Balm of Gilead. It simmered with thin, wavering resonance and carried those balladeer lifts that turn a melody into the forests and the streams.

Those saints who recognized the melody from Sammy Davis Jr.'s Billboard hit on the radio, or the striped shirt saccharine charm of Aubrey Woods in the film, hummed quietly along:

The Candyman can cause he sits inside the
world and wears a starless hood.

Mr. Muir rose from his chair. The children had gathered around
him when selecting their sugar sticks and Mr. Muir tapped their
little heads along with the playful bounce of his melody:

> *Who can play Canasta?*
> *Dominoes and Spades?*
> *Capture all your pennies and your seashells and your*
>   *shades?*
>
> *The Candyman.*
> *The Candyman can.*

Our new saint went on and on, gathering steam, slipping into
fable and legacy in the span of a verse:

> *Aurora Borealis.*
> *Sophia Albertine.*
> *Here we have the marriage of the cosmos and a queen.*

John the Revelator,
Alone upon his stone,
Pined for revelation from that gentleman enthroned:

    The Candyman.
    The Candyman can.
    The Candyman can cause he sits inside the world
       and wears a starless hood.

Mr. Muir pulled back the curtains of his talents. He regaled us
with the sorcery of his craft, commanding harmony and chorus,
like a spectral ensemble walked on the wake of his song, and it
was not his voice alone in that room but thousands, our saints
joining them, and none sang louder or lovelier than young Fleur,
who lifted her youthful, cherubic voice to lead this holy choir:

    Who can run forever
    from settlement and swarm
    like a little birdie who weathers out a storm?

And we all sang out, well-trained in the refrain:

The Candyman,
The Candyman can!

When his song had concluded, Mr. Muir stood in the center of our grand room, soaked through to the bone with sweat. As for Acacia, we panted, and what a painting we made, still as concrete, surrounding him in tableau. Every eye was fixed upon that cream-linen suit, the muddyless shoes, the green ballcap bowed across his waist, dangling from his crooked pinky. Applause began in smatters and did not sweep the room, for though awed, we were spent; the saints had sung out their souls.

The Nightingale then offered Mr. Muir the room opposite hers — the room she had occupied as a child; the room equipped for ceremony. And Mr. Muir welcomed the lodging. Declaring his lassitude, he asked with a measure of urgency to be shown upstairs. Given the man's grandness, this required a significant time to reach the second floor, which freshly presented an anomaly to all present, for he had recently paddled himself up the difficult inlet, and likewise held the winds of the Mormon Tabernacle Choir in his lungs, and so must, somewhere within him, possess great stamina. But such are the fickle reinforcements of Heaven, and even the diminished Samson required Heaven's aid to topple Dagon's temple.

The Nightingale chose Fleur and me to show Mr. Muir the way to his room. I carried his leather doctor's bag. Before we entered the long hall, he paused and waved at the saints gathered below with the protracted aplomb of a seasoned crooner.

The hall in The Pear House is long, and adorning the walls are paintings representing significant events of Acacia's founding. But as Fleur and I paused to explain each of their significance as had become customary on the first night of a new saint's arrival, Mr. Muir showed strong signs of disinterest, which soon devolved to fidgeting fingers, and finally outright agitation. I was perplexed. I had performed this service for several other arrivals and Heaven's guidance into Acacia always inspired a deep desire to understand our origins.

But Mr. Muir's intentions soon clarified. As I shared the meaning of the portrait of the Nightingale hovering above a lethal marsh, bedecked in a moth-eaten, emerald dress as porous as an ancient wyvern's wings, Mr. Muir asudden snatched up Fleur in his bulky arms and glided her down the hall with shocking speed, as if on rollerskates. When they reached the room equipped for ceremony at the far end of the hallway, Mr. Muir slammed the door behind him.

Though stunned for a moment, I followed at a run, and not far behind. When I reached the door, frantic sounds commenced inside — scratchings, heavings, and the screech of Mr. Muir's curses. Later, I would understand the racket was Mr. Muir dragging the heaviest of the furniture — the bed, the dresser, the desk — to barricade the door.

And I banged upon that door, in fear for Fleur. But all that presented was the eerie silence of the deep thicket. Mr. Muir's expedient departure also meant he'd left his doctor's bag in my hands. It was then that a profound lethargy washed over me, like I had succumbed to a hazy eddy and swirled at its whim. I thought of my father, summoning the strength to raise a tarnished spoon to his grey lips when his sleeping sickness flared, and I dropped to my knees, awash in the surge of my churning guts. Downstairs in the Pear House, agony resounded as many of the saints lost their stomachs and bowels. My eyes poured water and yet I did find the fortitude to open the lid of the leather bag of Mr. Muir. And I did peer inside before I lost consciousness.

Previously, rows of striped sugar sticks had been cheerily arranged in small Mason jars, strapped to the innard flanks of the bag with leather straps. I had seen them myself. I had selected butterscotch. But where the sugar sticks were once arrayed, the satchel had been emptied of treats and now contained only a cold, steel revolver.

The angel of death wears many faces. On that day, the elephantine Edgar Muir disguised his sickle with sweet diversion. A judgment for us all, but fulfilled unto death only for Salvatore and Delilah, who perished from their sticks of cinnamon and lime.

The saints awoke the morning next and found their feet. The Nightingale was gone from the Pear House, and our estate was in disarray. As we floundered, mourning those aforementioned whom we could not rouse, wondering if at last the Commotions had begun and left us bereft a deliverer, we did not spy the young being we knew so well enter through the back door and take root in the kitchen. Yea, we did not spy her, Fleur, with her white dress sullied, nor either the Nightingale—wearied from her eventide hunt for Fleur and Mr. Muir throughout the dangerous thicket—as they prepared a special broth of herbs, that they might pitch their wiles against Heaven and the angel of death and derail all that had transpired in the darkness of the woods.

After the Nightingale—fatigued as I had never seen her before—presented herself and Fleur to us in the great room, she bade us hush; she then guided Fleur to our table and sat beside her on the bench and fed Fleur a bite with a silver spoon from a gilded bowl as though she was not a young woman but an uncoordinated toddler, and likewise did she then comb and re-braid her hair. And only then—only when this peculiar meal was finished, and Fleur returned to a bed to sleep under the Nightingale's tending, such that she might work over her dreams and erase all trace of those horrors endured—did our bumbling swarm of bedraggled and shat-stained trustees of Heaven batter down the door upstairs and the furniture behind it. We knew Mr. Muir had already departed the night prior, but not from conventional exit, no; from the window—designed by Jolene Nightingale to give her daughter, Salome, the benefit of sunrise—and apparently in flight, with Fleur in his grasp, as the thick layer of dust on the inner and outer windowsill lay completely undisturbed.

BOOK XIV

*RETIRING from the STORY
& THE BEDROOM of the HERALD
& THE CONSUMPTION
of MY LITTLE BOOKS
& A NECESSARY SCOURGING
& THE MAJESTICAL RESTORATION
of FLEUR
& BEHOLDING the ORB*

The account of Mr. Edgar Muir inflamed the saints with fresh unease. Witnessing their demeanor, I was grateful to have revivified this crucial story, both in the absence of Fleur, as she recovered upstairs from her mauling, and as a reminder of the supernal heritage of her Boy who, as he often did, had slunk away unnoticed during my speaking. But for the rest of those gathered: What is a dosage of fear but the potential for fervor? For freshly lit passion seals a saint's allegiance. These stories of Acacia are our communion wine. We draw unto the bosom of Heaven and drink them deeply.

The saints prepared to retire for the evening. Scaling those stairs so recently detailed in my story, I made my way down the hall, brushing my fingers across the vast holes in the walls blitzed by my rake the night I had deposed the Nightingale, not yet repaired. For a moment, I yearned for what had lived here before. I lingered on and probed my hand inside the apertures of plaster, palming timber and nail, and I appreciated the strange textures as I did when I was a child and pawed the lingerie and nightgowns in the intimates section of Fayetteville's Sears.

Reaching the end of the hallway, I paused before the room opposite mine — the room I had just described from which Mr. Muir and young Fleur took flight into the thicket. Inside, Fleur lay, recovering from her wounds. I determined to check on her and gripped the doorknob. But a dark presentiment then did wrap its coils around my heart. I felt that to open the door was to again meet Edgar Muir — to witness the whoosh of his beating wings — to tremble at the creak and coo of his song — to find his doctor's bag refreshed of its deadly contents — to see him aim at me, Petra, his long revolver.

And so I turned away and toward my room on the opposite side of the hall. Removing the key from around my neck, I unlocked my chambers and therein met mortification.

Atop my bed sat the Nightingale's covenanted Boy. Before him lay the pile of my sacred little books, spread and violated, pages shorn and crumpled, their spines cracked. My little books, behind my locked bedroom door, securely stored in my cupboard. This cupboard locked with a key of one copy. This copy on my person.

Our eyes communed, and I struggled for the skeleton key to unlock his hold over me. The Boy tore a page and raised it to his mouth. I perceived then the pagan nature of his errand. He was eating my books.

Wretched, wretched Boy.

Vigor at once enlivened me. I strode to the bed and laid bare knuckles to the skin of his scalp. I hauled him to the floor, down the stairs, and into the garden. My anger roused the men with rakes, and they spilled forth from their rooms in the hall and joined me in setting upon the Boy. They stripped, slapped, mocked, beat, and spat upon him. And when at last he lay unmoving, they interred him in an inhospitable shed.

I returned to my room, shocked afresh at the despoiled pages before me. Atop the bleach of the expansive white duvet, I tenderly straightened out my disorderly pages, and then reordered their contents by history, and then made notation of which portions the Boy had eliminated in consumption so that I might recount their happenings later, and there, in some wee hour of my cataloging, I received visitation from Heaven. I opened to fresh pages and scrawled in my little books as though the night stretched eternal.

The morning next, I paid a visit to Fleur in her sickbed, meaning to tend her, but also admonish her for her child's act of violence. But I took special caution before doing so. Appreciating the natural defenses of the maternal bond, I intended to massage her allegiances, treat her with salve and easements, and in truth persuade her fidelity favorably. But upon entering, I was astonished. I found Fleur sitting up in her bed, sipping tea, and apparently entirely rejuvenated of her wounds. She briskly stood before me, shedding her nightclothes for my examination. Thigh and stomach, arm and breast, these had been horrifically marred before. Now, only faded scabbing showed.

What miraculous healing she presented; beyond the best medicine. Could she speak on what had passed throughout the night that she had been so wholesomely restored? Had Mr. Muir, whose presence in her room I had sensed, transmuted his deathly nature; did he now tend the infirmed? Fleur's responses baffled me. She seemed unable to grasp the nature of my questions. She interjected with nonsensical, contradictory logic and persisted in long-winded rambles that I might spare her child.

My ire intensified; she was a person of nonsense; of fancy. The punishment I had levied her Boy was commensurate with the child's offense — nay, even merciful — and not without precedent at all in the traditions of Acacia. Did she not comprehend the weight of his grievance? Did she forget that I myself had been the guest of honor in our sheds for vastly milder infractions?

Wearied by such fanatical pleading, and also feeling a great hunger, I left her room and returned to the hall. A sharp smell greeted me; a trinity: chemical, pungent, and nauseating. Something was amiss. For several moments, my fingers lingered on the smooth walls, and I could not determine what perplexed me so. It was only when I reached the staircase that the truth presented itself—overnight, the holes in the walls of the hallway had been repaired from the wreckage of my rake.

The main floor of the Pear House was empty. No voice, nor prayer, nor the bustle of a substitute for Fleur in the kitchen preparing breakfast. Grand lethargy. Impermissible quietude. I drew my shawl and sought my flock outside. But instead of a gathered group of sluggish saints, a monumental sight greeted me.

Only a skeleton had been there before; an outline; a vision slowly fleshing. But now, here stood the Nightingale's fully completed orb: sound, spotless, and shimmering. The orb was thirty feet wide and a steep fourteen feet high. Its architecture, a dome arching from the earth, was perfectly spherical, its walls without blemish. I walked around its perimeter, running my fingers along the brilliant panels. They were hot to the touch, and so terrifically bright that even the muted morning light made them difficult to take in directly. The entire structure was impossibly cruel, lacking entrance at any point, save the top. I slumped before the edifice, to my knees in worship involuntary, and braced my palms to the warming metal.

Voices. The saints of Acacia spilled forth from their morning worship in the chapel. They rushed forward and set upon me with kisses and then ushered me back inside the Pear House, thrilled to share the fresh wonders they had so recently fulfilled.

Dear Divining Reader,

As I came to understand, my night of slumber after Fleur's mauling and the story of Mr. Muir persisted for nineteen days. When I failed to arrive for breakfast the morning after the Boy's consumption of my little books, the saints broke down my door. Lamentations arose, for I lay twisted up in my sheets, soaked through with perspiration, my neck bent unnaturally and my mouth agape, and seeing these things the saints believed I had perished by some violence. The Son, however, drew courage and drew nigh, sitting beside me. He discerned the faint swell of my chest, the nearly soundless murmur of my lips, the still warm, though faint cherries at the peaks of my cheek bones. I had not left Acacia, the Son said, but was only deep inside the *terra coelum* of another trance. He emptied the room and disentangled me from the sheets. He laid me on my back mummy-straight and set a clean covering under my chin to mop my spittle.

On my nightstand rested the neat bundle of loose pages I had penned over the course of the night under Heaven's trance. The Son of the Nightingale could not resist stealing a look. He took these up and found them set in legible order and dated for that morning as though it was my breakfast order, filled out and tidy, and waiting for him to act upon it. This nightfall ledger contained my instructions ordering the completion of that special place of worship, the Nightingale's long-neglected orb:

> The saints will find the blueprints for the Nightingale's orb in the bottom drawer of my armoire, under the nightgowns. Complete the inner paneling and the outer facade of the orb to the nail — in accordance with these plans — with the silver panels the Nightingale acquired.

> Next, a carpenter is to construct a special structure (a ladder of sorts made of jointed beams) which mimics the angle of the orb — set on a heavyweighted cart so it may be heaved to and fro.

>🕮 Completing this, the carpenter will scale the construction. When he reaches the apex of the orb, he is to shear a hole in the panels at that uppermost point three feet in diameter. Then, the carpenter and three saints are to be lowered through the hole, into the orb's bowels, by a rope.

>🕮 Completing their work fortifying the interior walls, the carpenter is to ring a handbell. The carpenter and his men are to scale back through the opening of the orb. The men will leave nothing behind — not hammer, nail, canteen, nor rope, nor clothing, nor candle, nor lantern, nor foodstuff, nor tool of any kind, nor paper, nor any material supply.

Believing my writing a decree, the saints of Acacia occupied themselves by bringing life to my vision. Meanwhile, they took it upon themselves to patch up the ruined hallway while also tending me in my state of indignity.

Had they changed the sheets when I soiled them through nineteen days-worth of bodily excretions? Bathed me? Imagined me in states of intimacy, my hair free and my breasts discernible in such sheer and private nightclothes? And what of these written words of mine which they seized upon to finish this fresh wonder? Had they also perverted my cabinet when I sent them for the blueprints and found the private inscriptions of Petra? Like the Boy, had they despoiled my little books?

They witnessed me in disrepute. Enough to set my crooked lip with temper.

As the events over my absence were explained at our table, I ravenously set upon a meal of green peas, chard, eggs, and potatoes.

When I had finished, the saints petitioned me to regard the work of their hands. For beyond the building of the orb, I had closed my cataleptic writing with specific instruction revealing the sacred purpose of the orb.

It would hold the Boy.

The saints are to fetch the Nightingale's Boy from the shed in which he is confined. They are to carry him inside the carpenter's workshop. As Heaven provisioned the ram to Abraham, it will again be so — the Boy is to be bound to the adversary Heaven supplies inside that place by iron collars. Smelt those two collars from the graven iron beak of the chapel's vulture effigy, which is to be found in my second drawer, beneath my undergarments. When these things are accomplished, I will awake and provide to you the reasoning of Heaven.

BOOK XV

EVERY LIGHT LEFT LIT
& WITNESS to his CAPTIVITY
& THE COLLAR
& BEHOLD, the ADVERSARY

The dictate I'd wrought chilled me, like I'd plunged through sheet ice. Like I'd been swept up by its current and could only bang my feeble palms against a cold and unfeeling power greater than I.

The twitch in my lip would last for weeks.

I ordered every light in the Pear House left on — flashlights, the lamps and lanterns, and every candle, room to room, fired. I then turned to my own quarters. I expected Mr. Muir anywhere, everywhere. The hidden spaces of my room were searched, double-searched. I drew the curtain around the claw foot tub and peered behind it. I stood on my chair to examine the long, wood grain mazework on the top of the doorframe, clean from dust; I peered deeply into the metal mechanisms of the lock on my door.

At last, I collapsed to my bed, thinking of Heaven knows what, and the Son snuggled into my bosom while fever, sweat, and apparition vaulted through my consciousness, peppered with the replay of old country western songs, and memory flares, like my mother, standing before the farmhouse sink and scooping out bites of a steaming berry cobbler with her fingers, and my father, drunk in his white underwear, climbing atop our roof and claiming he could fly while my mother talked him down.

I contemplated Mr. Muir in all his possible guises, and when I'd meet him next. I imagined the Boy in the orb, a madman prowling just beyond our windows, stalking his prison like a starving lynx. A strain grew in his scrawny arms. Like Sampson, he may yet send our haven tumbling.

I sweated throughout the prismatic dread of night. I tried sleep and it outraced me. I tried diversion, patience, sex, even exercise, shifting the Son off of me for fifty jumping jacks in my nightgown before fatigue called my bluff. I tried indulging the liminal time of midnight, like I'd milk it for a sweet drop of honey on the tongue. And finally, I knew what I must do. I woke the Son. He lazily dressed with little protest. I left him to rouse several other trusted saints from their beds.

To reach the rooftop of the orb, my instructions had dictated the building of a special ladder, though it was closer, perhaps, to a curving movable staircase. Built with wide stepping planks affixed to a kind of rudimentary wagon, the contraption could be rolled back and forth with six pairs of sturdy shoulders.

Through sacred geometrical instructions, the ladder rested snugly against the camber of the steep angled outer walls, which otherwise could not be scaled. My trusted saints heaved this weighty curiosity into place. And then I ascended to its uppermost point alone. I did then lay myself down on the orb's subtle plateau to peer into the hole.

The Boy sulked at the western side of his prison. He looked a feral thing, the hair on his head now shags and mats and lengthened well-past his collarbone. He chewed the ends, mulling the tresses around his tongue like a cherry stem, and gazed upwards through the opening. He had shed his trousers.

Above me, a cloud drifted over the moon. I heard the cry of a raptor overhead and dropped my face against the cool tin. When I raised it again, the Boy had shifted. His shoulders arched and his head drooped between the knees. The cloud lilted on, and I viewed about his neck the totem of my dominion — an inch tall metal collar, one-eighth thick, welded sealed, but loose around his neck that he may grow in to it for a captivity undetermined.

Shame tremored through me. Shame akin to seeing my mother gripping the bare back of my crush, John Mosley, in my parents'

Jesper bed. But I did not share her prolific ability to live beyond the world-changing act.

Through me, Heaven had decreed judgment for the Boy. Through me. How my directives and the Nightingale's ambitions for the orb shared a twisted kinship. We were two collaborators cut from the same craven cloth.

I was culpable. I was soiled by the Divine, if such a thing were consistent at all.

In truth, witnessing him there, I wished to free the Boy. Even while I am liberated, even while I am the Prophetess named by Heaven, taking my meals where and when I wish, governing our haven, walking throughout the amazements of the thicket, brushing with fresh tubes of fluoristat Crest toothpaste, I suffered with the captive. I have been the captive. I have felt that weight of the greater power, like a knee in my chest until I could not breathe. But I perceived that releasing the Boy from the orb would prove a special kind of liability—it would nullify the order I had so assuredly evinced to the saints. It would negate the will of Heaven, and to contradict myself would surely strain their confidence.

And so instead, I watched the Boy deep into the night as he ambled about the orb. He raised his fingers against the cool tin, like a leisure hand from a car's open window. A sharp hiss then echoed somewhere within the orb, and I recalled afresh that my instructions had given mention to some counterpart to his captivity. The Boy swiveled his head. The chain that bound his neck stretched taut. I followed its length into the shadows, though I could not discern its ending.

The Boy stood to face his adversary. He gripped the chain and heaved. Hand-over-hand, slack chain pooled between his legs.

A lordly vulture breached the center of the orb, bound by a smaller iron collar compressed in the flare of its neck feathers. The bird spread its resistant wings to slow its pace. Its keen talons lay waste to the wild grass. It urinated down its leathery legs, caterwauling from its blood-red head.

Violence commenced inside. I privately marvel at celestial maxims — my ineffable proclamations — and their impossible complexities. Yet here I remain, steadfast, Heaven's vessel. I slipped out of sight of the orb's opening, determined I would return when I was not so mystified.

BOOK XVI

BAFFLEMENT of the ORB
& ESTABLISHING his COORDINATES

I watched him build coordinates within the silver maze.

Within the orb, the Boy understood no certain position. He studied the walls, palming the uniform perimeter in the cool of sundown—an effort to situate himself; to gain his bearings. But a night's dreams, and his bodily shudderings, and the moon passing overhead erased the coordinates gained in daylight and the morning-next rendered the walls silver and uniform.

When the Boy was small, Fleur perched him on her lap in her chair and taught him his letters at our table. At her urging, the men with rakes taught him the turn of the wrench, and the intricacies of the thicket's foliage, and the methods to hunt for game, first on the back of the Son's motorcycle, then on his own child-sized yellow-fendered Honda motorbike, which the Nightingale did privilege him to tour about alone as though no thicket torment could touch his sacred flesh.

Within the orb, the Boy recalled these lessons on the architecture of the letter. He generated a rudimentary method of orienting himself.

Head thrown back, he pressed a raw edge of his collar against the wall and ground the tin to his kneeling. Thusly, he accomplished a mark — a long letter *l*. Now, should dream and moon wash his memory away, dawn would find the marking true.

Dear Patient Reader,

During my convalescence over the nineteen days when the construction of the orb was completed, I was silent. But the final night before I woke and discovered the orb, I began to babble upon my bed. The Son of the Nightingale cleared the room and took notation.

I again include his writings to supplement my true account:

> Wrought with wretchedness and bodily convulsions, Petra opened her mouth and began to prophesy:

> —Mirror and deepen. [inaudible] Acacia has been decamped. A sheet stormed through with [inaudible]. The Earth shudders, angry, and alone. It would see peace. But peace is tugged across Heaven's boundary and drowned by the angel, Edgar Muir. These last days [inaudible] set before me, only a haze, while the figurines of Heaven are flying, trampling. Blurs veil in our bodies. [inaudible]. Acacia will meet Heaven. My saints, when you wake, will you find that you can run?

If only I'd recognized the sedition maturing in Acacia. If only I'd sniffed it out like a marsh hound and bayed until I fainted. If only I'd leapt inside the orb and raised my rake to the Boy's head myself.

BOOK XVII

AN INTERPRETATION of PROPHECY
& THE BOY
MANAGES the GROUNDS of the ORB
& CONFRONTATIONS with the
ANTAGONIST
& LABORING for SIGNS of MERCY
& HEAVEN'S CAPRICIOUS WILL
& A SHARING of DREAMS
& THE CHURNING of MY BODY

The Son wished for me to explain this prophecy. In his exuberance at hearing me speak after so many days of mindless stupor, he had witlessly shared my augury at our table. This proclamation of mine concerning the Commotions, and the security of Acacia, and the revived peril of Mr. Muir had horrified the saints.

I would clarify it for them with certainty, I told the Son, and the following morning, for it was time again for me to observe the Boy.

During my extended slumber and for a duration afterward, severe drought beset Acacia. The inlet wasted to a trickle and the soil cracked and separated until the mud flats resembled scales. Our crops withered into skinny brown totems and many an animal wandered into our vicinities to lay its head down and die. The wild grass sprouting from the layer of soil above the concrete foundation of the orb likewise died entirely. This spiny bedding agitated the Boy's skin and made him as cross as a feral dog. But the Boy grew resourceful. He discovered that if he apportioned some of his rationed water to the soil, if he concentrated it in a patch, just drips and not a deluge, the buffalo grass and the sandbur would after a measure of days revitalize. Heaven blessed this effort, and in scant time a sprout of green bedding became his portion. He laid on it with his limbs spread wide, like the man in that famous drawing from the art books in Jolene Nightingale's library. There, he took in the sun, the stars, and my cloaked form above as I lay on the perch of the orb and lowered him bread and a jug of water.

The Boy would secure this water to grow his linens. Like a gladiator performing for a bloodthirsty crowd, he gathered up a length of his chain and wielded it as a whip. But seizing their rations only initiated new heights of ferocity in his adversary, the vulture, who screamed and fled back toward the walls, keeping the chain taut and cumbersome for the Boy as they circled each other.

And so, the Boy did then court strategy and introduced a few scraps of food and small pours of water into both of their bowls, though a lesser amount, in order to preserve the lion's share for his grass.

Witnessing their struggles, I crawled under my bed and labored to receive revelation. Heaven, I asked, deem it just that I increase their rations. Let my hand be your banqueting table. Let them suffer with their stomachs full. And illuminate this prophecy, this mess I uttered, concerning your final advent. Unscroll its parchment. Suss out its hidden language. Give me its meaning and may the saints be edified. And toward the latter, I did receive what seemed like guidance, for there are a thousand ways to enter the spider's web of prophecy, and no reason to begin at its densest tangle.

We had assembly the following morning. Fleur arrayed a splendid breakfast on the table—heaps of buckwheat pancakes and honey, wilted greens, potatoes, sausage links, and orange juice from cans of concentrate. I stood at the head before my chair. I had prepared carefully how I would speak.

My portent had agitated the saints, but not simply for its inferences to the calamity of the Commotions, for Acacia understood that this precipitated the final advent of Heaven. No, it was for how it stoked the saints' fear that Acacia had somehow displeased Heaven; that we would be excluded from its mercies in such a hostile judgment day to come. Therefore, I prepared nuance and encouragements, a joke or two, an anecdote of our founding, all hopeful uplifts to spread like burn cream over my incendiary words. But when I stood before the saints to speak these soothing things I had prepared, Heaven removed the control of my tongue and I personified only a doomsayer; a mad sibyl, calling in the wilderness. And what I said was this:

—The evil hour nears. Acacia will see the Commotions three years hence. Consume while you may. Have you arrived at this table for your final meal? Take pleasure in the yeast. Suck your bacon fat of its salt. An angel of ruin alights the currents, swift as the comet, seeking whom it may devour. In these times, starve yourself as you are able. What pagan fills their belly while their soul wastes? Eat if you must, but in haste. Mr. Muir nears, and blood will sluice, huckleberry friends, wider than a mile.

I then collapsed into my chair, bewildered at Heaven's commandeering of my tongue, and I wished the cushion would swallow me whole. I had no intention of making any such pronouncements, only that I might be a soothing balm. The saints, meanwhile, observed me with a torment so thick I could have sculpted it like clay, they a simple collective who wished only for vacancy of care and creature, for Mr. Muir's cold shoulder, and for infinite soft bedsheets and a gentle leader to lay them down.

The Son rose from his chair to intercede. He spoke with measured tones, winging his words away from the wreckage of my short sermon. He encouraged our place on earth for such an interval as this. And he opened up our gathering with an invitation that the saints might share their dreams.

Isabella stood.

In her slumber the night before, she had observed the corpses of many animals on our grounds — oxen, pigs, squirrels, foxes, the black headed ibis, and the old-world sparrows. As numerous as hailstones dotting the acreage, these had been slain without any sign of wounding. They decayed before her eyes at an unusually rapid pace — like a month-long timelapse played in a handful of seconds — as fur and feather, flesh and cartilage, organs and bones withered their matter.

After Isabella, Johannes spoke of his dream. A white room, empty of everything, where a small white ball, not much larger than a marble, rolled slowly across the floor, gaining mass as it progressed.

Then Tomsen told of the murder-sound of cicadas — a brood that blackened the windows of the Pear House. A man in a baseball cap stood on the porch. He snatched a cicada from the air and bit its shuddering carapace in half.

Our table waited on me, for I was expected to explain the significance of these signs and wonders. Interpreting the saints' dreams was my well-worn wheelhouse; my number one hit. But instead, I had only a bodily response to give.

Under the table, beginning at the thigh, my legs crossed over each other. My upper foot coiled around the ankle of my lower leg. My elbows did then place themselves on the table before me, and my arms did then weave around each other, and my wrists too, even my fingers on each hand, crossing as though defying a vow. And then my tongue did also twist in the closed prison of my mouth so that I could not form a word. In my chair, I bent about the waist, although my neck efforted a turn in the opposing direction. And beyond all these wild contortions, I was beset upon by a fit of absonant laughter. It was a sound contralto and forced, as though from my bowels, and obscured to grotesquerie by the misshapement of my mouth; the mirth wrung out of me like Heaven's dirty dishrag. The Son lifted me up, carried me to my room. He laid me out on the bed where I continued to cackle and writhe. No visitation appeared to me. No reveling assurance, nor grand elucidation. I had the mind and spirit of any normal person, and with them could only observe the humorless fits of my voice.

The Son tended my face with a washcloth until my howls turned to snickers — and my arms relaxed and unwound — and my fingers released their tension — and my legs uncrossed — and at last my body lay flat. Wrung of vitality, I gave in to the slumber of the deep.

Dear Sympathetic Reader,

Of the events which took place after this humiliation at the hand of Heaven, chief among them ranks this, for it is now that I will recount for you my careful unpacking of the Nightingale's chest—concealed beneath the chapel—an unarchiving which I had resisted for a time, perhaps because I sensed the irrevocable de-mazing such discoveries would provoke.

Yet still, at last I drew on the wellspring of my vigor and produced the Nightingale's briar Dr. Grabow, and brewed a strong black tea with thicket herb, and committed myself to the contents of her chest:

From the chasm of that dented vintage trunk, I pulled out trinkets and totems, dried flowers and rusted skeleton keys, quill pens, cigar bands, and Joe Cocker cassette tapes, and also her drafts of sermons, and a napkin drawn with an articulately rendered maze in blue pen. There were small bottles of oil stopped with cork and a wad of Clementine post office receipts bound with a hair tie, still containing the Mother's wisps. There were several early volumes of my precious little books, swiped from my sheds for their prophetic insight when the Mother found herself in a dry spell. There were my beloved pinstripe overalls, still carrying the dried grime from my arrival to Acacia, and in their bib pocket, the maze from my father's book. There was that contraband Colt revolver of Mr. Muir's too, a ruddy cowboy gun with an extra-long, thin barrel, carefully wrapped up in the handkerchief I had worn around my neck, a memento from the good woman, Ava Caldwell. I did hold that cloth cushion and that gun in either hand for a long moment, feeling their equal weight as though I, Petra, were the scales of justice, before wrapping them back up and concealing them in my dresser. And in the bottom of the chest, underneath the faded pig-belly pink of a whoopee cushion and a stack of the children's crayon drawings of birds, it was only then that I found the true substance of Acacia in a bundle of loose-sheaved parchment; the clandestine archive that the Mother had not shared with me those years before in her private garden.

The aged pages had been bound with a tender piece of lace, like a present in a Hallmark commercial. Fiddling the bow loose, I laid them out on my bed. Each was filled with the orderly cursive of the Nightingale's quill—indented and loopy as expected—the ink pooling where she paused too long, constellating in the white sky of the margins.

Reader, we arrive at my life's greatest revelations, and I labor to pen them even now.

First, Jolene Nightingale—the foundress of Acacia—had expended a much greater portion of her fortune over Acacia's early years than I had imagined. The structures she had built, the fine materials for the Pear House, the largesse of so much imported furniture, the enormous pantry stocked for the end of the world—it had dented her reserves. But a mystery yet lingered, for the coffers I had found in the Nightingale's hidden room, tucked under the farm table against the bare soil wall, were full—even lotto winnings abundant. Where had these riches come from? What sustained us beyond the spent estate of Nightingale Lumber? Who provided our muslin for dresses, and the iron for new rakes, and grain and canned goods when the garden fell short, and the gas generators, and the tin panels for the orb? The benefactor shook my soul. The riches of Acacia had been supplied by my father.

The Nightingale's careful ledgers illustrated the story. At each point of diminishment—as Acacia's funds ran direly low, as Acacian bellies fed on root stretched to sinew stretched to imagination—there arrived a deposit postmarked from Llewellyn Caldwell. The funds balanced Acacia's books; restored them to solvency. Both in recent times and the distant past, as the Caldwell farm trudged along when I was a child. Many days our family missed a serving of morning gruel before our glory in the fields (lapses that filled the stomachs of Acacia with bread, pork and eggs, television sets, books, and board games)—this was not because our farm did not produce. In fact, it thrived. It was because Father was penny-wise and pound foolish; because he carried a primary allegiance; because he robbed Peter to pay Paul.

For every harvested red-wheat crop sold in Jesper and the markets beyond, the profit was tendered here, Acacia.

For every cent pocketed with his keen skill at cards, the winnings were tendered here, Acacia.

For every acre of our land mortgaged in hard seasons, until the corral of gentry drew close enough to zing it with a stone, the proceeds tendered here, Acacia.

Collected and packaged in greeting cards, Father sent our earnings south to a post office box in the nearby town of Clementine, Texas. There his missives waited for the arrival of a truck; for a saint costumed in western duds, guided through the thicket by the Mother's hand-drawn maze map, who turned a key in Acacia's lockbox and retrieved her tribute.

Llewelyn Caldwell, my daddy, altruist of Acacia.

I rarely spoke to the Nightingale of my parents. Only toward the end—when she took joy in hearing of my family's vexations. Nor had I ever had opportunity to ask my parents what they knew about Acacia. Inquiries which now smoke of foolishness.

Why? Why would my father expend such excess on Salome?

Heaven provides a lamp in dreamscape and darkness. I uncovered the depths of the diseased affinities between our houses in the final pages of the Nightingale's account, carefully prepared, as if she knew I would someday uncover it.

I had a brother, older than me by scant years. He played in the garden before I toddled the earth. Learned his figures first. Toured the grounds, repaired a threshing machine. Learned the manual transmission of a truck. Advanced before me in bodily pleasure. Found himself sprawled under the stars, drunk on fermented Acacian wine.

I had a brother. And the Nightingale's writing revealed it was the Son. For my father, Llewellyn Caldwell, had been one of those early wanderers drawn to the grounds of Acacia. Present for the betrayal of Matthew Paxton, it was he who lifted Salome Nightingale from her imprisonment in the shed, from beneath the blanket of mice martialed by Heaven. Once she had matured, the Nightingale took Llewellyn as her swain, and it was Llewellyn who made her a mother in our earthly sense. For a duration, the Son, their union, sutured them together. But my father was spirited; turbulent. The Nightingale suggests in her writings, ineligible as her helpmate. In time, she began entertaining other suitors, and this enraged my father.

Under the cover of darkness, Llewellyn departed Acacia. Heaven preserved him through the thicket with a straight, wide path, well-lit by the moon, and free of foe and fowl. He established himself north, in Jesper, Arkansas. But no sooner had he won his fortune at cards and leased his fields on the outskirts of town, and bedded Ava, his new wife, than a gnawing began. A knowledge. He recognized his error; he was fashioned for the place he'd shunned.

Llewellyn poured forth written pleadings to the Nightingale, dispatching them to Acacia's postal box in Clementine. He could no longer taste salt, he wrote. His toilet ran liquid. Intimacy with his wife produced no release. But his letters met with no response. Llewellyn took long drives back to the Lake O' The Pines, plunging into the thicket and seeking an entrance to his former home. He planned every manner of convincement: he would grovel before her, Salome, naked in the soil, and plead her grace; he would steal into the Pear House in the dead of night and throw her over his shoulder like they did in *Seven Brides for Seven Brothers* and blitz-krieg his way into the thicket to renew their vows in front of a chorus of flaming-faced vultures. But Heaven had sealed Acacia within the thicket, and he could not find his way. Llewellyn redoubled his efforts, sending a flood of earnest letters scrawled in secret from his woodshop or the cab of his truck — he had a broad-shoulder, and it belonged to her, squared to the abyss, he wrote — and who else but him could hold up a mirror to her memories from girlhood, like when Jolene Nightingale had asked him to buy water balloons for a garden waterwar for her fifth birthday, or those special words she'd muttered in the tongue of the dead when he'd lifted her to his shoulder on her only tour of the sheds — and besides these things, he pledged her this: his everyday labor, the bounty of his capable hands. If his servitude took an age, so be it. Jacob labored for Rachel, and so would Llewelyn for Salome.

He received but one letter in return — a lonely salvo in the cavernous roadside mailbox at the edge of his property, a copy of which the Nightingale had preserved for her archive. Llewellyn must have rushed to his workshop to break the seal of this letter with quivering hands, and his exhilaration must have then been met in equal proportion with devastation. For it was a short missive, written in algid, pragmatic language, and free of scent, and sentiment, and memory. Heaven, Salome wrote, did not see fit to restore him to Acacia. And beyond the Son he had abandoned, she said he ought to know, she was advanced with her second child. Heaven assured only he could be the father.

Father's lodestar had flown. He would never set foot in Acacia's boundaries again and the ache bound him to a lifetime of bitter penitence and unending tribute.

Here, I perceived the cruelty of Heaven. Windstorm swept through my biology; a revolution in my cells. I knew it all, even as a I learned it word by word by word; even as the Mother's account returned me to my origin.

The Nightingale wrote in her journals of a difficult pregnancy. Of a demon child who vexed her. She vomited often, and she felt insatiable cravings for chili dogs, and she went into labor prematurely in her bedroom quick as an electric shock where her saints held out their hands to receive the Mother's girl-child, bellowing, bemoaning, her transit from womb to world.

The Nightingale then wrote of the orders she had given to the trusted Acacian man in the western shirt in this memorable act of vengeance against the man who had betrayed her. The saint separated the infant girl from the brother who watched over her bassinet and drove the babe from Acacia in a woven basket set in the floorboards of a blue truck. The saint passed through Jesper under a murky moon, slowing at the four-way to let law pass first. Three miles hence, the driver turned the long slate driveway of Llewelyn Caldwell's growing magnanimity. Sounding the brass horsehead door knocker, he left the basket and fled the steps, concealing himself behind a weighty tree.

Petra the Wretched, Queen of Dirt, exalted by the Caldwell's porchlight, swarmed by moths.

—Bounty of Heaven, Ava Caldwell cried, as she lifted me from the wicker basket—Llewelyn, see what Heaven has wrought us.

And only a decade later would Ava Caldwell reverse this course under my father's duress, sending her own girlchild, Fleur, as Llewellyn's tribute—swallowed in a white lace thriftstore dress—in the same wicker basket in which I had arrived, back to the swallows of the thicket; and thereupon, Ava did, with weeping, don the leather harness Llewellyn had made for her, and for a while yet, continued to present to Jesper as with-child—all to protect the good name of our fallen patriarch, all to satisfy the angry pact he had made with Heaven, all to forestall his wrath, and perhaps somehow even earn again his astray affection.

But she did not go un-mourned, then or now, not Fleur, a daughter, my sister, a lost little flower, traded for a stone.

Heaven, if I love, I do not love thee. I am my father's mirror—my lover's apple—my sister's thorn—the Prophetess Mother's dagger. I have plunged from the sky; I am disastered in the scorch. I can write no more of these things. I include instead a portion of my earlier writings, when the promised Boy was long-imprisoned in the orb, and in my soul I encountered him, cared for him. Not as a mother. As a stepmother. Just as the woman, Ava Caldwell, despite her simplicity, had defied my wayward origin and called me daughter and gave me home.

BOOK XVIII

CONTINUED STUDY
& A TEASE of the RAPTURE
& DISCERNING the SPIRIT of the BOY
& MANNA from HEAVEN

Cataleptic at the revelations within the Nightingale's chest, I kept as steady a hand as I could manage on Acacia while I continually watched the Boy; watched over intervening years as his upper lip began to sprout, and his sex matured, and his body took on the limber of a younger man's frame; watched as he developed the mazework of his silver cell; watched as, with the *l*- mark at his back for grounding, he studied the curving wall across the orb; watched how he paced the expanse under the moonlight and along the chain, stretched straight across the orb's distance, grinding two *ll*'s into the silver wall by the collar at his throat; watched as he thereby predicted half the distance again along the circumference of the wall in order to cut an *lll* into the metal; watched as he danced toward his adversary across the chain yet again to make his crossways mark, an *llll*.

Because a trial without the hope of relief produces little benefit, one evening I tested him. I dangled the Rapture— that thickly knotted rope from the Nightingale's swing (removed from the tree for this purpose)— into the orb. Tied securely to the cambered staircase outside, I hiddenly hoped it would be feared.

But it was not.

Hand over hand, the Boy climbed the Rapture. His was a strained ascent, weathered as he was, but not without some spirit left in his arms. I lay on my stomach, mostly out of sight, until his head crested the edge.

He met my gaze with the certainty of a death rattle. The Commotions he'd someday usher-in sounded like a chanticleer at dawn. I should have knocked him on the head with my rake. But instead, I reached a hand for his mangy face, perceiving that he carried the voids of Heaven's citadel, and in that communion the compass was swallowed up, and the hourglass tipped to its side, and the scale was broken. I have no memory of my bodily will. I held my rake— and the rake rested its iron flat against the Boy's forehead— and the rake pushed steadily, not so he would fall, but so he would lower himself down the thick knots of the Rapture and return to the recesses of the orb.

The Boy's adversary greeted his descent, hopping on one foot on the patch of grass, cooing gleefully like a demoniac cheer-leader under Friday night lights. Returning to the Pear House, I ordered the Boy's rations increased by a jug of water and an additional cut of meat, and this within earshot of Fleur, so that she may perceive my goodness toward her child.

When I visited him next, it was in the dead of night, and I carried a sack over my shoulders. The Boy slept, but the sly eyes and brooding hisses of his adversary showed it awake. I fastened the Rapture to the staircase and descended into the orb hand over hand.

Above me, my brother, the Son of the Nightingale, waited to extract me if I was set upon with violence.

Heinous evil had conceived this unordinary shed. I had not been inside it since the Nightingale toured me through during its construction. I set down my sack and crept to the walls and palmed the prison she had conceived for me. Even as the animals in the thicket called out and the whispers of the Son sounded at the orb's crest, I shut my eyes and heard their echoes swirl within the bewildering acoustics of that place. Here, the rescuing whistle of the train would torture from every direction at once. How could I ever have answered its call?

But wisdom had fashioned in me a good sound mind. I could leaven the bread of even the worst of the Nightingale's torments.

Standing in the center of the orb, I opened my sack and cast forth its contents—an abundance of small orange and white pellets— like manna from a drunk and flush Heaven. Then I scaled back up the Rapture and stuck my tongue in the Son of the Nightingale's mouth and then shooed him off so I might maintain my vigil.

Daybreak. The Boy woke to the welcome morning drizzle. He rolled from his patch. He held his silver bowl to the sky under the orb's opening and drank his fill and crossed to the *ll* section where he dumped a portion into the bird's bowl. He then turned to study the thousands of pellets I had deposited, scattered about the earth like a sinking constellation, and he the deity that oversaw their arrangement.

Thirteen days later, there sprouted the first bloom of purple violets. The Boy pet them in the glow of sunbeam. Soft clover then did flush, and buttercup, followed by bursts of friendly chamomile. The Boy lay among the earth's release with his arms extended, savoring the blooms in his mouth like a box of fine chocolates.

Defying odds, the patch of flowers spread beyond the circle of my distribution. They infiltrated the undercurrents of the soil and diffused through the tunnels of earthwork with their tiny tendrils and blossomed throughout the orb and then beyond, into the garden and the grounds of Acacia.

The goodness of my hands, not Heaven's.

BOOK XIX

THE DAY PROPHESIED DRAWS NIGH & THE DESIGNS of a DEPLETED WILL

Dreadful. The day I'd prophesied years before in my sleep spell neared. Acacia braced for the arrival of the Commotions.

And yea, over these years, the saints had grown greatly vexed with my preparations. They deemed them vastly insufficient. I did not disagree, but I was restrained by forces beyond my understanding, for when I roused myself to order the reinforcing of the Pear House, or that the earth be dug for shelter out in the grounds, or that an inventory be taken of our canned goods, or that water be carted from the inlet to be boiled and stored, my tongue stiffened in my mouth like a gravestone.

Otherwise, I was able to speak. I interpreted their dreams and discoursed on scorched earth and starvation and the awesome destruction of Heaven's final advent. But fortifying Acacia? In this I found a phantom. I found the only task I possessed will to complete was to watch the Boy.

Whose resolve was stronger? Mine or Heaven's? I am capable of violent intercession. I could outwrestle Jacob, a weak-legged man. I could piledrive his angel and hock spittle in its mouth. I had sundered the foundation of the Pear House with my screams and driven in the Nightingale's skull with my rake. I had blessed the Boy's comfort in the orb. And I had only so recently commandeered the saint's devotion, tilling the barrows of their belief so that they might flourish in the starglow of my leading.

And this birthed in me a solution. It was true that my fugue state prophecy of the Commotions had already been issued around our table that day when I wound myself up with all the elegance of a state fair pretzel and discoursed against my will. I could not revoke that sorry event. But should it come to pass somehow— should the Commotions arrive as I had said— then I would be affirmed. But if it did not— if the day came and went without any sign of cataclysm, without a drop of blood, or siren, or screech, or violence, then Acacia's confidence in me would surely waver. I could not risk such a thing. In these uncertain days, and with their temperatures already so raised, the saints needed no occasion to find me a candidate for their rakes.

Thus, I determined to preoccupy the saints in pleading with Heaven that it change its course. As I would explain to them, the falsifying of my prophecy would mean that, at least for a small duration, we had received an extension on Heaven's mercy; our strenuous worship had earned us this benefit, and Heaven's debt would be collected some other day.

And so, I called for the saints to assemble outside the Pear House. There, betwixt an eerie air, as though Mr. Muir nearby prowled, I instructed in the strenuous appeals that, if the saints performed them righteously the following day, and if we were found without blemish, just might sway the fury of Heaven.

Dear Pardoning Reader,

I interject in this presentation of my little books to reinforce the distress in which I thought up this contrivance and all that follows. But in the interest of my true account, I include it so the reader will discern that even I, the true Prophetess of Acacia, is subject neither to divinity nor absolute will, but that she is like any of us, only chosen for her role, and composed of bodily flaws, and occupying a house of fragility. She may, in seasons of impairment, stumble. But Heaven's plan is secure and overcomes our lapses, and our momentary shortcomings are no diversion to its implacable will.

BOOK XX

THE FLAGELLANTS
& THE ASSUAGING of HEAVEN

Early morning, and the sun already sweltered. We joined hands around our table, and I led the saints in a prayer for fortitude. I reminded Heaven that we had been faithful— I reminded Heaven that we would demonstrate said faith— not with the vain repetition of words— not with hollow handiwork— not with holiday fits of spiritual commitment— but with sincere atonement. We ate a simple breakfast of bread and butter and took in a good deal of water from clay pitchers. The saints then undressed, leaving their muslin in piles on the floor, for naked we came and naked we shall return. Together, we crawled in a moaning mass from the Pear House, going across the garden on our bellies, and past the orb, and to the chapel, where we interceded for Heaven's charity until past noon; until the sun reached its highest point above our hermitage. Afterwards, I ordered a small barrel of water be brought forth and each of us satiated ourselves with a mouthful from a long silver ladle. I bade the saints outside. Crawling to the orb, we surrounded it and stood to our feet like Joshua's outmatched army.

We rejoined hands and commenced in unison a mighty, wailing plea— may the Commotions be delayed! We basted the orb in our terrors and confidences, in our fantasias, and in the terrible, fascinating joy that we might meet Heaven's Golden Purifier.

Our fervor reached its crescendo and then melted to embers. We released hands, and I took stock of the saints, panting, delirious, as soaked through with sweat as if they'd just emerged from a swimming pool.

We had the ear of Heaven, this I assured. I passed a towel to the Nightingale's Son. He wiped his hands dry and gave it to the saint next to him, who did the same. We've been invited to the inner sanctum, I shared. The towel continued its rounds until each saint had unmoistened their palms. Let Heaven hear.

I then instructed the saints to step up to the orb and place their open palms against its blistering surface.

Our collective howls burned like incense. They carried the deep— a sign of good faith that made an absurdity of all these recent petty trials. They were an offering I affirmed Heaven heard as I circled behind the saints, exhorting them with my rake.

The day wore on as our wails diminished. Many Acacians had lost consciousness, and others the will to stand. They slumped around the perimeter of the orb like trampled flowers— Tomsen in a heap of slick, flabby flesh— and the Son prostrate on his stomach— and Alice, flat on her back, her bare feet inches from the orb.

And from inside the orb, the frenzied sounds were unyielding. We carried on our worship blessed by the potent screams of the adversary, and the Boy, who beat his palms against the walls, braying in a frenzied tongue I could not discern; a sound amplified by the interior geometry of the orb and forced through its root hole with the unnerving resonance of a perverse megaphone. I professed their racket efficacious of the saints' effort; the throes of Heaven, beaten back.

When our day of prayer had concluded, I summoned the broken saints back inside the chapel. I tended their seared palms with salves and bandages. I massaged their flush shoulders and kissed bloodshot eyes and blood-raw cheeks. We broke communal bread and cooled our throats with ice water. When a peculiar peace had at last attained, I spoke quietly, in near-whisper. How blessed we were to complete such a straining venture, I said, for we had that day secured the mercurial favor of Heaven. The Commotions would be withheld— at least for the time being. However, I cautioned, we mustn't slacken our dedication. Not for a moment. To do so now would remove us from the shadow of Heaven's wings, and I could make no promises that Heaven would not renew the date it had previously ordained.

The saints received my message with a hallucinatory gratitude and collapsed afresh in embraces and simpers of relief. I bade them then return to the Pear House, where they stumbled to their beds like a mass of the undead for strange dreams and short slumber.

And when the day of reckoning I had prophesied came and went, and the sun rose as normal and descended likewise, and no tempest, nor plague, nor hailstone, nor brimfire, nor vengeful Boy, nor Mr. Muir in one of his many guises visited us, I ordered a celebratory feast be prepared for the saints.

Our bond was strengthened; for most, not all. For like a silent flu is passed to another through the lip of an unwashed glass— like perfect vision deteriorates in the hegemony of an eclipse— like a handbell's ring fades its sure salvation, I sensed the festering of insurrection.

For several saints lingered in passing, sharing hushed words in those near-after days. They cast prolonged looks at the orb,

pressing an ear when they perceived the coast clear, to determine, I mused, the state of the Boy inside. At supper, these were
the ones whose heads bowed for prayer but whose eyes never
closed, and I recalled anew the statue's beak left on my plate,
now melted down and shaped into the collars worn by the Boy
and his adversary.

My thoughts turned to the affectations of Matthew Paxton,
who had persuaded the first saints of Acacia against Jolene
Nightingale. I would see like things in my tenure; like the distant scent of a corpse plucks the scavenger's nostrils, I sensed it.

Dear Watchful Reader,

In prudence, I began to take my meals in my room alone. I ordered my brother begin secretly tasting my food before I consumed it. Weeks later, my wariness was justified.

It was a Monday night, balmy and gentle, with little thicket rustle from bird, fox, or boar. After our triumph at the orb, a stillness of heart had attained among the saints; a placidity, like Heaven's afterglow. The saints occupied themselves on the main floor of the Pear House, playing Hearts and Jenga and helping the children make origami frogs from the set of used orange Childcraft books. For my respite, I shed our muslin dress and wore a comfortable lacy slip I had found in the Nightingale's trunk and watched this week's *Alf* on the television in my room. The reception fluttered, and I rose and spread the antennae's fingers like a peace sign. I stuffed my pipe anew with tobacco and returned to the bed. With just my feet, I peeled off my socks one at a time, pinching them between my toes, stretching them out, and catapulting them to the floor. I could have been an ape. An electrician. A hippie. I could have been so many things had Heaven spared me its affection.

My brother carried a tray of food into my room. He set it down and then sat on the foot of the bed, blocking my view of the television. He began to tell me a story in earnest about a small rabbit, for that morning, while working in the garden, the rabbit had hopped up to him and sat on his rake and refused to move. He picked the small one up and carried it back to the edge of the thicket. It was a charming coney, he said, ashen black, with big, bubble eyes. It hopped away, then paused and looked at him with such a peculiar stare that he followed it into the thicket for a time, through amazements and thorny quagmires and pathways, not realizing that the rabbit had drawn him in such short time to the exterior of the thicket's reaches where Acacia bordered the imperiled world. Peering beyond the final burst of bramble, the Son saw a road. He took a few steps after his curious little escort, then a few more, and the blacktop of the country road warmed his bare feet. The Son thought about taking a walk along the road. How far does a road go, counting its connections? he asked me.

There is no stop. I know this now. Only a rerouting, even if it's back from whence you came.

It was a small story, and the last one he'd share. I hardly listened, to my unending shame, instead adjusting my head against the pillow so I could watch over his shoulder as Alf fell victim to wrongful censure for a cat who'd gone missing.

As he concluded his story, my brother performed his duty; he cut into the meat pie meant for me, spearing a bite of the flaky crust and smushed peas and stringy brisket and creamy gravy, and consumed the mouthful.

Short minutes later he perished at the foot of my bed. The Son carried the small almond vulture eyes of the Nightingale, and I retain their final condition— bulged and bloodshot, sluicing tears. His creamy neck, smooth and fragile as the penis bone of a racoon, wrought with gibbous, straining veins. And worst of all, the denouement as I soothed his exit in my arms— the sweet running brook of his voice, garroted, like his throat was a quarry and he gargled pumice.

I did not cry out for him. Why, I do not know. The saints made crafts and deployed their strategy to shoot the moon in Hearts while in the cave of my bedroom, I relished his death rattle like a sugar stick I would not share. I let him down from the tight sling of my arms into the satin ocean of my throw pillows, and then, imbued by Heaven, I took up the poisoned pie and strode downstairs.

To all the saints gathered there, I sang out of this fine delicacy— the fragrant onion, the seasoned brisket, the peas, perfectly mushy. The best meal I had tasted in years. We must have this twice monthly, at a minimum, I said, prepared exactly this way, down to the grain of salt. Performing so, I keened who watched me with anticipation as I bit into the pie, then consumed the entire thing in ravenous buffet.

As you know by now, dear Reader, my body is a temple, fortified by an infected Jesper bouquet and a serpentine Nightingale tongue. Heaven has built in me resistance; Heaven has fashioned me a purifier. I returned upstairs, but far from the Son's ghastly death, I suffered only a turbulent stomach; a gurgling cod.

The following day, I sunk into a bubble bath to release my grief, drawn for me by a trusted saint. My temperament vacillated between sorrow at the Son's passing—he, the grounded pyre around which my years of anguish and accomplishment had been tethered—and rage—at the quisling saints who had removed him, the only jewel for my warm sentiments. I slicked back my hair, and my fingertips caught in my curls, and I pulled at them until my vision wavered. My hand went for the hundredth time to the crook of my quivering lip, which the Son looked beyond to call me comely. When he carried me this kindness, said I was lovely, it affected me so that if he had asked, I would have braised my heart and fed it to him with Neapolitan sorbet.

I saw my bathroom through a heavy haze of tears. The water I soaked in was murky with soap bubbles. Still, I perceived that a tannish-colored limb now swirled gently between my naked legs. I imagined that Heaven had sutured the Son into me—that my principal body bore a shadow—that I carried his organ. In that perplexing moment, I reached forward to squeeze the appendage. My motion aggrieved an entity, for it was no celestial joining of our bodies, but a young water moccasin, smuggled into my bath by an agent of schism. The viper surfaced seamlessly from between my legs. Angered at my touch, it slithered upon the length of my outstretched arm and struck me on the cheek. I grasped the serpent by its small diamond head and wrenched its fangs from me. I did then sunder its body like a handful of dry spaghetti. And with the severed, bloody bits floating before me, I laid out my reckoning.

The day next, with my cup of coffee at the dawn, I dressed to perform the first funeral rites for my brother. I found the inner sleeves of my quilted ceremonial dress irritating, itchy, but I went about raveling my hair into a puffy fishtail braid and then tended my eyes with heavy Maybelline. Still, the excitability against my skin persisted. I peered inside one tight cuff, at the moth-eaten purple lining. Citrus, pungent, nauseating. The fabric was dusted with a thick white powder. I peeled back the neckline of my dress to reveal the same. When I had gathered a small amount between my fingers and rolled it into a ball, I took hold of a sparrow perched on my open windowsill and raised the morsel to its beak. The bird seizured and perished almost immediately in my palm. I let it fall out my window and into the flowers below.

I set upon the offenders as an avenging angel.

Tomsen, this beloved old saint, I ordered dragged to the steps of the Pear House. I disrobed from my ceremonial dress, and naked again before Acacia, forced him to lick the inside of my garment. He perished in the same grotesque manner as my brother. Alice, I ordered stuffed into a barrel and nailed shut inside. At the bottom, a dozen venomous hatchlings coiled. Her terror satiated me. Sarai haughtily lay her head upon the stump in the chapel and this I stove in with my rake. And Stephen. For Stephen, I rendered punishment as his namesake was so judged. The smallest stone was cast first—a pebble the size of a thumbnail—so that his agony was great.

Purging these conspirators produced an exodus. Seven more apostates fled during the night, braving the terrors of the thicket where they undoubtedly met their just agony.

Though I suspected her beyond all the rest because of the imprisonment of her child, I could not touch my sister, Fleur. I wished her banished, imprisoned, crucified. But I could not muster any smidge of evidence she had betrayed me as the others. Fleur was fresh-faced and covered in flour always; she carried sweet treats on a gilded tray, derived from florid imagination and inspired ingredients. She was faithful in the chapel however I commanded, the first to her knees, and the last to rise. By every indication her worship was fervent. If I was the hearing trumpet for some word from Heaven, then always she was my bullhorn. One evening, I concluded our services early and visited Fleur in the kitchen. She was a steady whirlwind of practiced expertise. Bedecked in a frilled apron, she tended simmering silver pots and cast-iron skillets and so many spice jars arrayed before her like an artist's oil paints. I watched her for a while, and then I requested she bring my supper to me in my room. Ample time to season the dish with any of her misadventures.

A short time later, she appeared at the door. She had dressed for the occasion in fresh clothing. She was meek, and lowered her head as she entered, pushing a bar cart bedecked with an array of Jolene Nightingale's finest silver serving platters and their shining, domed cloches. She sat on the edge of my bed, in the same spot as my brother had. When I asked if she had tasted the food, she assured she had; it was her way always, since a dish reflects its maker, and a good regard toward the work of one's hands is worth more than costly perfume.

I beckoned Fleur serve me. She scooted along and placed the largest cloche on the comforter. When she bent to unveil it, I lunged, spilling the earthy dish across the sheen of the bedding. We grappled for just a moment before I took a strong grip of her wrist and elbow, wrenching her arm behind her back and forcing her face to the sheets. After she had calmed, I bade her open her mouth to chew, which she did, nibbling among the strewn cabbage and stringy beef. I discerned carefully as she digested the meal with nary a mal effect. When she had swallowed several mouthfuls, I released my hold and let her rise. I offered her a hand towel to clean herself while I ate what remained of the food she had prepared for me.

The walls of memory serve when besieged, buttressing one's defenses with a lifetime of fear and grievance. But when I had finished that clean meal, glutted and secure, reclining against my fringed pillows to converse with the pretty young sister before me, I did then let down my drawbridge, and charged with the energy of an unceasing storm, my soul did then spill out. I gave to Fleur every word. About my sorrows of the passing of the Son, revealed to her then as my brother, and our unaware union on account of my vengeful expulsion as an infant; about my stumbling into Acacia with my father's mazework map and the vulture's leading, when that handsome soul first greeted me; and of my penthouse suites in Acacia's torture sheds; about the Son's hidden swimming hole where we made love, and the deposition of my little books, and his quiet affirmations of the uncanny beauty I carried in my face; and about the Nightingale's hidden account I had found in the room beneath the chapel and all of its unwelcome divulgences. And of course, savoring the final revelation for its disastrous implication between us in that moment, I at long last shared with Fleur the twisted kinship we held as daughters of the banished saint, Llewelyn Caldwell; of how I had mourned her, my sister, my flower, my stone, all those years ago in Jesper, only to find her now before me, alive and well. I had little expectation of her sympathies, nor her camaraderie, not that we might braid each other's hair and play MASH and bicker over who got to wear a prized dress like spoiled Jesper debutantes out for the likes of a boy like John Mosley. But when I had finished this torrent, and raised my gaze, and met her red-rimmed eyes sincere, I did then marvel at the wisdom she shared with me in that exchange. Simple, yet profound, truths—that we cannot control our origin, or our love. The Son and I had raised each other up, entertained the prism of a bond few if any could fathom. That she and I shared a similar union. While she could not live my grief, she would sit with it; sit with me; sit with him, tucked, cold and swelling, under the comforter beside me and topped heavily with fragrance to ward off the putrescine. I warmed at her faith; at her sisterly love as we embraced. I would not harm her. I told her so and swore it with our hands clasped as I wept. Likewise, her child, imprisoned at Heaven's whim; so long as Heaven stayed its hand, I swore to her I would not kill him, this uncanny flesh of my flesh.

The required three days of keeping the body of my brother warm passed. Heaven did not return his breath though I interceded it be so, though I laid my lips to his and wept and beat his pale, white chest where the faint scars of my nail-driven shoes still showed. Alone with him in my room, I shaved his hair, beard, and body and trimmed down the nails of his fingers and his toes. I brushed every nick in his skin with salves and bathed him in frankincense and melted our white candle wax over his eyes, mouth, ears, and anus.

Robing myself in a simple frock, I rang a bell for the saints to bear him from my room. Our women waited for us on either side of the hallway, their candles lit. Fleur blubbered as I passed. She tried to embrace me, but in this time so lost, I could give neither her nor the saints the benefits of my sorrow.

Before the garden, the body of my brother was placed upon a palanquin of acacia wood, chiseled on its side-beams with murals of the vulture in distinct stages of its nature like avian stations of the cross: in hunt in the sky, and feasting upon the dead, and perched atop the largest Acacian shed. We lifted my brother up and passed by the orb in solemn procession toward the chapel. When we reached its doors, which did seem warm in their welcome of this solemn ceremony, we set the carriage upon the ground. Several of the burliest men with rakes scaled the walls with ladders and took their post atop the flat roof. On the ground, saints affixed ropes around the body of my brother and in short time he was hauled to the roof of the chapel. I laid down and was similarly bound and then pulled up to the roof to sit with him. The men with rakes then rejoined the saints below, leaving me alone with his body. The saints joined hands and started up our song of arriving and departing; our delicate, our swerving, "Moon River."

This was how we sent off our dead. A ceremony unbearable when the deceased I loved. I would not raise my arms. I would not pray. I would not cross the body. I would resist Heaven and all its maze of commandments. I would dig my love a goddamn hole.

But Heaven ever thwarts our weaknesses. Even as my soul was in revolt and I determined to change course and have my love carried down, they appeared over the trees. They keened the scent of the cadaverine. Two at first, then six, then a dozen. Circling on the drafts, they eyed his meat, beaks agape.

BOOK XXI

THE LOSS of MY DEVOTED
& A SCAPEGOAT to DRAW them OUT
& DESCENT into the ORB
& A JOINT VISITATION to the
BANQUETING TABLE
& THE THRONE ROOM of HEAVEN
& THE UNION of HOUSES

Acacia, sturdy and solvent; Acacia, an empery distressed.

I had lost my most trusted confidant, the Son, dispersed to the bellies of the birds, and through my tenure, a few saints I thought beloved besides, and I spent days of grief, of wilderness, meditating without ceasing atop the orb. And from that metal bastille, my suspicions magnified—for insurrection is achieved through a strong coterie, never disconnected, never in silo. The heavy armoire covering the trapdoor to the hidden room in the chapel—the serpent striking me from the bathwater— the sleeves of my garment—the Son's meat pie. I had purged a handful, but among our hundred, there must be a larger portfolio of offenders. So be it. I would set the thicket ablaze and flush them from hiding. I would do so by testing their mettle with their countersaviour, the promised Boy.

The Boy waited for his morning breakfast. But for the first time, with a bounty of smoked ham and a heel of rye bread tucked inside the wicker basket, I did not lower the Rapture.

The sun declined, the light lovely and silty gray, and as customary, I returned to the orb. Men with rakes watched me from the chapel—women with candles witnessed me from the windows—and again, I refrained from lowering his basket.

The subsequent morning, again, no rations were supplied. The Boy sat crosslegged in the bloom of his flower garden. The chain draped from his iron collar and looped off the knob of his bony shoulder like a feather boa. He glowered at me, toiling the sprouting hair above his sex.

That noon, a storm broke and the Boy stood with his head bent back as rainwater filled his mouth.

On the fourth day, the Boy grew faint. He masticated live beetles in the flower garden. He sucked morning dew from the grass.

On the fifth night, he shed his shirt.

And then, on the sixth morning, I mounted the stairs and lowered the Rapture inside the orb and descended to the ground. In truth, despite my fury, I could no longer stomach this treatment; this help and harm, coursing through me, the same vessel. Every day I looked less like Petra and more like the Nightingale.

This day, I brought him his basket, and I unpacked the meal Fleur had prepared for her child: slices of cheddar cheese, a bottle of apple juice, a crust of bread, and thin cuts of cold beef. The Boy ailed against the western side of the orb, while cooing its interest, his adversary hopped over to join me in the grass. I fed it a fatty piece of meat.

In time, the Boy crawled over to join us. He drank from the juice I offered him and nibbled at the cheese. The flowers inside the orb had thrived, and the Boy broke off petals to flavor the crust of bread. I set about trimming his hair and the scruff on his face and then bestowed him a new blanket, which I did then lay out beneath the hole of the orb to lean back on my elbow, and I did then beckon him to lay beside me. I stretched my toes to their peak and felt his feet brush past my ankle. We peered into the thick clouds beyond the orb's aperture. I sang to him softly about the rainbow's end, and reached over and pulled his body closer to me, nuzzling his face against the crook of my jaw, which did then alight my lip with a furious temper.

And then together, as if winedrunk in the dizzying dew hours of homecoming night, we crossed into Heaven on the bridge between worlds.

❧ Heaven

Born into the brume on a vulture-drawn chariot, the Boy assumes the reins and steers us beyond the clouds. We pass through strata of vapors—hazes of thick, pea-green mist and reflective, black opal empyrean foreboding, softly stirred by the vultures' wings—until at last we plateau in the vast, pillowy plainsland of the upper reaches of Heaven.

An infinite vista lays before us, free of cityscape and vegetation. Only one structure stands to speak of: a grand banqueting table. The table is wide as a country lane and built of smooth plank, thick as railroad ties. It stretches into the distance like a painter's vanishing point. Around the table, the souls of the world have gathered to sup. The souls occupy transparent bodies—like trophy casings—which sit straight in their highbacked wooden chairs, hands clasped, and heads lowered as if saying grace. Within each gossamer body, a trapped soul of the earth seeks escape from its form, sloshing throughout the extremities of its fingers, neck, and legs, like the red-blue-and yellow tinted bubbles in the liquid-motion toys at the kiosks in the Fayetteville mall.

I perceive that at the head of the table, alone at the end of an improper eternity, sits a copy of the promised Boy who has driven me to this place.

With a crack of the reins my Boy pilots our chariot upon the great tabletop. The rush of the vultures' wings extinguishes the long candles, though by the glow of the seated souls' illumination, I did then witness Heaven's stagecraft:

The Boy bears a long-handled Acacian rake. Leaning from the chariot, he wields it in opposition to those souls lighted red. He smites the chamber of their bodies and their fermenting essences inside into wisps, until we reach at last his duplicate at the end of the table. Like a casino deck rapidly shuffling, the celestial cast before us carries a carousel of forms flickering within its confines, and I see—my brother, the Son—then Salome Nightingale—her mother, Jolene—Llewelyn Caldwell— the foretold Boy—Fleur—myself—and every handmaiden of Heaven that has served Acacia from genesis until now. The false carriage grips the burnished arms of its velvet chair until its fingers crack the frame. Its mouth lets out a scream and the tongue's pink casing transmogrifies in two paths like a forked serpent. Raising up his rake, the Boy strikes down this abomination, splitting the thing in half and spilling its soul fluid about the table like melted wax, the odor unwholesome as a charred field of stinking corpse lilies. The Boy then lashes our vultures away from the table and tours me throughout the landscapes of the spheres; through phosphorous rivers dotted with smooth stones the color of red wheat; through expanses of blank white, where thicket whispers from the light years of my past—*locus terriblis, lusus naturae, hortus conclusus, puer natus est nobis*—pummel me with ghostly fists.

Starbursts brighten a space in the vapor. We ascend further still and make our way to a wide road paved with small, glimmering stones. The Boy reins in our vultures and slows the chariot to a walk. Above us, tremendous crystalline waves ripple, separated from the deep caverns of terra firma. Within these passageways of fish, and somnambulant seaweed, and porous coral, the drowned populace of earth lithesomely float. A lacy yellow substance trails behind each body, like the death train of a Jesper wedding gown.

And fascination turns to deeper mysterium, for before us looms the Pear House.

As we draw nearer, my understanding of its construction matures. This is not the Pear House of my rule, nor even of Salome's tenure. This is the *inceptum finis est*—the first estate of Jolene Nightingale, foundress of Acacia. The establishment— and this I grasp in full for the first time and grow immediately numb—of my own grandmother; of my lineage.

The estate presents as sharp and pure. A mirrored replica of what I steward but purged of every dark angel's ambition, and rebellious contrivance, and season of bent scepter. We dismount the chariot and ascend the steps.

The Pear House is empty of Acacia's bustle and carries the eerie silence of a sacred ritual; a silence so vast it swallows the footfalls of the Boy ahead of me. And in that atypical quiet, my ears attune to a new, distinct frequency—a ceaseless murmuring—a nauseating drone—like the lowest note on Heaven's cello bowing without any moment of return. I fixate upon it as it reverberates, as it expands and metamorphoses before me into something veritably tactile. The impression of my ruin. Sound I verily wade through.

We climb the stairs and enter the Pear House's long hallway, the portal of Acacia's legacy. Paintings decorate the walls as before, but these differ from the Nightingale's tenure. In one painting, a rectangular work of vibrant gouache, I witness the Nightingale painted as a child, poised above her mother, Jolene, on a bed in the Pear House. The Nightingale's small back arches unnaturally, and her chin tips skyward, and a long, silver-handled knife with a curved blade is raised in both hands above her head.

The next painting shows the Nightingale, again as a child, on Acacia's grounds in the still of night. She wears opaline nightclothes and bears soil in a small silver pail en route from the garden to Jolene's room, where she is building the natural garden for her mother's corpse to rest.

In another scene, I discern a detailed bird's eye map of every turn of the thicket. A thin spooling of silver thread dangles from a bubble of clouds at the apex of the painting. It runs throughout the labyrinth's arteries, avoiding its pitfalls, and revealing every convolution. I see myself rendered a number of times within the thicket's densest tangles during my effort at escape: hiding myself under leaves, bathing in mud, and scaling the thin bark of a loblolly pine. I see too, the very hand of Heaven leading renderings of my brother along the delicate thread to uncover me and haul me back to the Mother.

In one section of the hallway there are portraits of my betrayers—those saints of Acacia who have renounced me—painted on small canvases set within inordinately large rose-dusted frames. There is Tomsen and his thinly trimmed, pointed beard. And Sarai, haughty as a great horned owl. Alice too, bashful-eyed but determined. And Stephen, who carries his namesake in this portrait too, resigned in celestial dignity of body and spirit. This series is a revelation to me. It was not simply my harsh treatment of the Boy that aroused these saints so, but more, their burning desire to establish him in my place.

A final painting is unfinished. Rather than depicted on canvas like the prior works, this composition stretches half the length of the hallway and is rendered on its raw walls. The surface has first been treated to a gold-leaf basecoat. Then, a webby mesh of cheesecloth has been stretched over the gilded facade, which patinas when I scratch it with my thumbnail. No figures adorn this painting; no abstractions, nor sprawling landscapes, nor portraits, nor languid nude alfresco picnics—there is nothing but a large, white, blurry circle that doesn't appear painted to the background so much as it hovers above it. We step closer, the Boy and I, and when we near, the circle grows in magnitude and intensity; an abysm that will blind me if I bear it any longer.

I know it then, and not with earthly comprehension—I know it with the lightning strike of the deep—the circle holds the Commotions.

All these paintings I wish to study, to benefit from the full measure of their revelation. But the Boy takes me by the hand and pulls me past the Commotions and toward my bedroom— my mother's room—my grandmother's room—at the very end of the hall. Chamber of horror, matricide committed twice therein, though I have no children to carry on this bloody lineage.

I grasp for my room's iron key, kept always around my neck on a cord of rawhide but find it missing. I signal this, but the Boy ignores me. With thumb and forefinger poised to pinch whatever he is fishing for, the Boy reaches deep into his mouth. His jaw then does unhinge considerably, and from the depths of his throat he produces a great key cast in silver which unlocks the door.

Inside, I expect the grand bed and billowing white comforter shared by the legacy of my house, and the walnut armoire that locks up my personals, and its top drawer that stores the

Nightingale's pipe and tobacco, and the small television angled on the nightstand on which we once watched Matlock solve his small wonders in the courtroom. But nothing of this Pear House resembles my fought-for tenure.

Within my bedroom, my sanctuary, awaits the throne room of Heaven. A blistering, majestic space, the room greets me with creamy pillars, snaked about with teeming vine, that support an impossibly high ceiling. Vultures circle about its reaches; feathered blips that swoop to the ground so I might perceive their red faces before they rise again on some vaporous eddy. In the middle of the room, where my rug should be, sits the judgment seat—a wooden chair, simple in design, and stained colonial maple like so many in the Pear House, though its backrest has been sculpted into finely carved wings. Next to the chair rests a small table carved from a stump. A sizeable book bound in leather sits atop it.

I understand the Boy wishes to introduce me to the seat. I should not be so fearful. Has Heaven not named me its champion? Here is oracular communion beyond my wildest expectations. Haven't I, devoted bondservant, executed every charge faithfully? I wish in that moment for finery—that I might pick out a trendy dress from Goodman's Mercantile in Jesper, or slip-on Thessalonia's red heels, or even don a crisp denim shirt, turquoise bolo tie, and the Laredo boots of my father, or best of all, be clothed elegantly with the layers of spectral light in this uncanny place.

But when I look over myself, I am ashamed. I am to greet Heaven naked, adorned from the womb.

The Boy approaches the throne. Like a thousand blocks of dry ice swell in unison, the mist of Heaven enfolds him. I lose sight of his frame, but his feet, these I can yet see—bare, cracked, and caked in grime—as they rise from the floorboards of the Pear House. He sucks the hum of that place into his lungs like a hurricane draws in the tides. He cries out for Heaven's final advent in the language of the dead. Pressure overwhelms my chest and wetness floods from my body like I am being squelched beneath Heaven's heel. The sound renders me to my knees, my forehead pressed to the floorboards.

Though I have ventured so far into celestial realms, I know I will not this day behold the face of Heaven.

When I returned from the bridge between worlds to the late afternoon of Acacia, to inside the orb, I found that I had coupled with the Boy. He lay beside me spent and slumbering, limbs sprawled wide among the wildflowers. I dressed quickly and rang my bell—the signal to pull me up. When my saints had done so, and not a single of them would meet my gaze, I understood I had spent the full day in the orb, and that our carnal union had been a quarter peep show; every throe and terror.

Dear Generous Reader,

My little books have now arrived at the day of fate. Baffled by the experience of this vision, by my affinities with the Boy, which I knew as transgression and curiosity and ecstasy and shame, I sought solace in my room. Alas, had I only that moment fled into the thicket when no shed contained me and I yet held the consecration of the saints.

I include now the final entry in my little books, composed on the night of the Boy's liberation.

BOOK XXII

POISONED and INDISPOSED
& TWIN SIGHT GRANTED by HEAVEN
& THE PENETRATION of the ORB
& A RESCUE
& A CULMINATION with the
TERMAGANT
& BEARING WITNESS to the ESCAPE
& IMPACT with the EARTH
& THE FOUNTAIN from THE STONE

Mortification. My trusted saint, Jacob, would not keep my indiscretion from *his* trusted Clarice. And Clarice's rotten mouth from the whole wide woods. I spoke to no one else and called for dinner upstairs, alone. I fidgeted about the room. Every trusted item of diversion — my television, my pipe, my wardrobe, my bath — was bitter in my mouth.

I put on Joe Cocker and gave in to vengeful dancing. I jumped on the bed until I slipped and whacked my head against the headboard. A half hour later, Fleur knocked on my door to bring me roasted root vegetables on a tray. Her head was tipped low, like she sensed my angst, my disarray. I took the tray and barked at her to leave and reclined against my throw pillows to eat. And against my best judgment, I returned to the bewildering sensations of the orb. The winged chair — I could build this. This was not beyond me. The gallery in the Pear House, explaining so much hidden lore of Acacia — I would commission these portents be created by the careful brush of Mya. And the chariot, borne by vultures (an earthbound facsimile would do) — I would construct this also and, drawn by donkeys, the children of Acacia would tour the grounds on holy days and board-by-stone-by-ceremony-by-song their joy would rebuild this place.

Finishing my dinner, I felt warm, anesthetized, as euphoric as time spent too-long in a hot spring. I turned on the TV—*Alf,* a rerun. I swirled back toward my bed, stumbling around in a wide half-circle, then regained my footing, as though a competent dance partner had stepped in to rescue my misstep.

I pulled the covers to my chin. Saw Alf toss his bangs and ruin a chicken dinner. My bed was bigger than a bed. Or perhaps I was smaller, like a sanguine infant cozy in the lulling citadel of a bassinet. My eyes rolled back as an unseen hand billowed me. I tasted burnt sugar. And all the while, my ears attuned to a dull consistent sound, like the antique tolling of a well-weighted clock. I was cognizant of my body. I fathomed my breathing. I could see straight ahead—the sheet on top of me, the comforter above it, my toes peeking out on the other side, and the TV beyond. My mind was sound, but my body resisted. I was benumbed, as though a vicious night hag with the girth of an anchor perched upon my chest. For my apothecary had at last extinguished. Or by some bespoke sorcery had been overcome.

I sat with the moment in sounding clarity as Fleur reentered the room. With a face as blank and hard as stone, she removed the key from around my neck and proceeded to unlock my armoire, which she did then rummage through for a few choice items from the Mother's archive, bestowing them, though I could not see what, in a leather satchel. She then looked upon me, and I upon her, before she soundlessly left the room and closed the door. In perfect concentration, I understood her and every machination. Fleur, she was a woman of many stripes — mother, a saint of the Nightingale, conspirer, poisoner, my sister — each allegiance longstanding, ferocious, and thorough. While she may have felt incapable of murder any longer due the shared bond between us, if my limbs had had any vitality left, I would have dispensed with the pleasantries. I'd have simply dragged her from the kitchen by her hair, taken up Mr. Muir's revolver, and shot her dead.

Heaven granted me a small mercy — a psychic privilege. I had known it only once before on the day the tempest razed Acacia and the promised Boy was born. From my bed, my sight ripped away from my immobilized body like a thin lid peeled from a sardine can. I went forth with rushing, as if on a rollercoaster, and at Heaven's behest I rode — under the doorframe, and across the hallway, and into the Nightingale's childhood bedroom, and out Mr. Muir's window, then over barrows of the garden and toward the orb — a thing unscalable without the staircase, but no match for the nimbleness of Heaven — and up its steep camber, and through the hole at its peak and into its inner-most — and soon, I was with-sight and in-spirit with the Boy as he leaned against his *L*-wall.

A blow reverberated throughout the panels; a strike against the outer side of the orb, but loud enough inside to blanch the brain. A second blow, then a third, and at last the wall pierced inwards, just above the Boy's cocked head. The sharp spikes of a rake glinted there, ugly in the moon's illumination. And then it was gone. Replacing the rake, the serrated blade of a handsaw stroked into the orb and razed downwards until it touched the floor. Inside, the orb grew as quiet as ancient ruins. The Boy charted his bearings and leaned his ear to the workings outside.

When the noise rejoined, Heaven redirected my vision to the exterior of the orb. There, Fleur labored with the saw, beginning again at the puncture wound and heaving another arcing line downwards. When she reached the ground, she began tapping the orb's walls with her hash-slinger touch.

I reentered the orb. Pressed to the wall between these two cuts, from which the moonlight did glimmer like a profane stained-glass window, the Boy responded with his own taps, slow and practiced. A language. They shared a language, developed under my very watch. I had sympathy for secret tongues. For any mother's intervention.

The Boy then backed away as Fleur threw herself against the weakened opening, rending the metal inwards; a childbirth *in principio,* the mother entering the womb, as the depleted wall delivered her in a heap inside the orb. She then rushed to her child and set upon his face and matted hair with furious kisses, producing afterward a canteen from her satchel which she held to his lips. During this tenderness, she touched the collar about his neck, feeling for any weakness in its forge.

Fleur then drew a potato sack from the belt she wore around her waist. Gripping the thick chain from its slack on the ground, and with a mighty heave, she hauled the Boy's adversary from the reaches of the orb into the moonlight. The vulture blinked, then fixed its stare upon the panting woman in this forsaken womb. It folded its wings to docility. It bowed its ochre head.

Fleur then walked upon the chain as if to keep it taut and pinned to the dirt. When she drew within a desirable distance, she crouched, paused for a breath, and leapt, capturing the vulture within the sack. She then slid off her belt and bound the creature tightly about its girth, afterward continuing her tour of her child's collar. But she found no sign of weakness.

—There is no time to remove it, she said. We must go.

The gaping hole in the side of the orb resembled a paper cutout, and a proper cosmology of hallucinations. Beyond the ragged edges of its shrapnel, I saw silver ore like the eureka windfall of a mining expedition—I saw the last rites of a man on a wooden bed, his bony hands collecting around the priest's collar, pulling the clergyman to a kiss—I saw my ruby Formica table set with gruel on mismatched place settings, and in the center, my father's leather book, open to some covenant that, if I could only read it, would surely reveal all.

Heaven then showed me the escapees—showed me Fleur first. She carried the sack holding the vulture. She stumbled into the garden and dropped the bird, then rushed and reclaimed it. Ahead of her the Boy hobbled, using a rake, recently stained with blood, as a crutch. As Fleur caught up to them, the chain dragged in the dirt behind the two with a looping mark, wide like a tractor's harvest. They made their way into the grey muck and wild grass of the thicket. Each of me — in vision in the orb and voice on my bed — tried to raise alarm; to summon my saints. But Heaven tended me now. I watched, and I was inept.

Fleur struggled. The belt which bound the bird had slipped, and the flex of the vulture's wings tested her hold.

My vision flashed outside to a loyal saint, Michael, who stood night watch on the grounds, slain by Fleur's rake beside the orb.

Two hundred yards into the thicket, Fleur and the Boy reached a small clearing. They rested a moment, nursed the canteen, huddled together in an embrace. The Boy seemed to regain his strength. The feral crouch he had so often adopted gave way to plank-straight shoulders and a heaving chest. He stepped apart from his mother. Fleur offered him clothes from a backpack which he declined. And then finally, across an eternity that wounded me with each interstitial moment, I heard the ringing of Acacia's bells within the Pear House. The coup had been discovered.

An ardent saint rushed down the hallway. Sonorous steps. My door splintered inwards. I could hear him, Mateo, but I could not respond. He heaved my body up and over his wide shoulders and then carried me over the threshold of the Pear House and out to the orb where the saints had begun to gather around Michael, whose head bled out in the dirt, his tunic also maimed across the chest.

Meanwhile, my spirit witnessed the desertion of Acacia.

Fleur and the Boy went across a defoliated opening and made their way toward a fluttering strip of yellow fabric tied to a single white sapling. Reaching the marker, Fleur left her child and continued walking until she reached a bloom of tall grass. A dozen yards further, she raised up a dirtbike hidden in the meadow and wheeled it back to the Boy. How canny. Had any of the good saints discovered the peculiar yellow marker, they would have stopped there and returned to report it to me immediately and not ventured further to find this means of escape.

I felt a swelling in my gut, like a helium balloon inflated near to burst. Heaven at last restored the power of my voice. I beckoned the saints close and whispered where we would find the Boy. I told of what would follow if he were not captured, for I knew that Heaven had leased him to unfasten the Commotions.

Heaven split my vision yet again. I was with the saints, yes, who had lifted my slumping body onto a wooden chair and carried me forward like a queen on her gilded palanquin as we rushed into the thicket, but my second sight remained before the rend in the orb. I peered into its abysm as though it was a jagged, silver-edged television that served me its choicest programming of the deserters.

Out in the clearing, the Boy kickstarted the bike while Fleur held it upright. The Boy climbed on. Fleur kissed him and gave her child the canteen and placed the vulture, no longer in riot against the sack, on his lap between his body and the handle-bars. She then pooled the excess chain over his naked thighs and embraced her child with the enveloping purity of captivating love. Perceiving this—even as I wished to split her in half—I wept onto the shoulders of the saints who carried me, and wildflowers did spring from the grama where my tears landed.

Heaven nearly saw us through. Our party reached Fleur just as the Boy's dirtbike left the clearing and penetrated back into the far end of the thicket.

A dozen vengeful saints fanned into a semicircle. Fleur turned to face us. From within the satchel she carried, she removed Mr. Muir's contraband long-barreled revolver. She held Ava Caldwells red handkerchief in her other hand. She looked to the thicket, where a blip of the dirtbike's dirty exhaust yet lingered. The handkerchief, carrying all its legacy, sagged its weight, and Fleur raised the gun to her head. The saints rushed her. One threw a rake. Top-heavy, it went awry.

A kiss of smoke did then rise from Mr. Muir's revolver, and Fleur gave up her body. I bade the saints carry me close. They laid me down in the soiled dirt beside her. Heaven returned the agency of my hands, and I palpated my sister's wet brown hair and searched her eyes for the secrets of profound immolation. I knew so many mothers; I had so many besides. What cavern in Fleur's soul swam with such unclouded waters that drawing on them powered the maternities of sacrifice? I sucked up the theatre of memories that toured my grieving mind. Of Ava Caldwell, the woman who raised me, teaching me cross-stitch at the table at our farmhouse. Of Miss Jensen, ushering me inside from recess and away from the torments of Carolynn Peters, and the half hour we spent sharing a Wonder Bread cheese sandwich. And I knew my Mother Nightingale afresh, every tenderness and every horror captured in this writing and those many transgressions not recorded.

Touching Fleur restored vitality to my chest, and I found the strength to sit up. But instead of discoursing with the saints, Heaven blessed my dual spirit and carried my vision high above the thicket where it allowed me to perceive the Boy.

The Boy rode with bewilderment at the before and after of the orb. The memory of the controls, the ease of throttle and clutch, the tenderness of the front brake, and the balance of speed, all these returned from his lessons as he broke from the substantiality of the thicket and found his way out of Acacia and, for the first time in his life, onto the country lane.

Entrance to the wider world traveled him a century of the senses; one of pavement, mile markers, roadkill, and bubble-letter billboards that advertised fuel and food in Clementine, Texas, twenty miles hence.

The vulture had rested while the Boy navigated the tumultuous terrain of the thicket. But with steady road beneath them, it located a negligible weakness, for near the pluck of its beak, age had frayed the integrity of the sack. The vulture worked up a small hole in the weakened burlap lattice, then plunged its beak through. It widened its maw and spread the aperture.

When the hole had increased sufficiently, from a fraction to a dime to an inch and then wider still, the vulture wrestled its red bald head out into the sticky morning air. Wind beat eyes. Frantic panting issued from its beak. With a violent wretch, the vulture vomited and the spew whipped over its head and around the collar and the feathers of its neck, and into the face of the Boy.

Still early morning, Acacia's two expatriates passed only one truck, and this headed in the opposite direction. It slowed to the shoulder, the driver ogling, as the dirtbike rode by in their lane.

The Boy shifted gears and increased their speed. The bird elongated its neck, straining against the sack to peck at the rusted metal crossbeam of the handlebars. The Boy ground his teeth. He aimed a strike at the bird's skull with his head. He missed, and their iron collars clanged together. Vision wavered, and the bike swerved, slowed, and bunny-hopped off a mound of dirt on the shoulder, but the Boy regained his certain hand of their exodus.

A friendly hand-painted road sign said:
>Clementine - 10 Miles;
>Come for the Kolaches,
>Stay for the Smiles.

They went at an even pace. A fast and low-volume gear. The vulture calmed. In place of protest, it steadily picked at the loose threads of the sack still restraining its chest. Tearing through a particular stitch, the old sack split an inch down the front. The bird flexed its chest and the sack unraveled down to its talons. The belt that had bound its wings shifted under the bird's contortions and slid down to drape the gas tank.

The Boy grasped the meaning of the bird's effort. He released his left hand from the clutch and reached for a choke of chain near the bird's rufous throat. But the vulture stooped its shoulders, and its neck drooped low, and its bristling feathers fanned like porcupine quills to prohibit him.

Clementine neared.

The bird spread its wings, magnificent and ash-black. It perched atop the silver gas tank. The Boy stood up on the pegs to view the road above the bird's shoulder, letting off the gas, gingerly pressing the rear brake with his right toe.

The bird sensed a draft, an East Texas whispering wind that soothes nerves and livens old flames. Wingtips fluttering, it leapt for the heavens. The Boy scrambled after the chain with his clutch hand. He caught its link as the vulture ascended, but near his own collar. Slack in their bind, the vulture soared a dozen feet above.

For a moment they rode this way.

The Boy stepped hard on the foot brake, efforting the bike to a stop. But the vulture veered left too soon on a gust of wind, ripping the chain from the Boy's hand. It went taut. The force separated the Boy from bike. He spilled off, onto the shoulder, rolling down a small incline and into an overgrown ditch.

Weight and chain and collars connecting them, the bird tumbled from the sky.

The bike flipped, rolled, and disappeared from the road.

At my behest, the men with rakes carried me back to my bed. I lay like an old, wounded general there, comprehending a nearly lost cause. But I had some fight left yet. I drew them a map from memory of Heaven's painting with the silver thread and ordered the men with rakes take a truck to recoup the Boy at the mile marker I had witnessed him fall. If Heaven did not confound me and blessed their exit, they'd find their way through the thicket.

Before the hour had expired, they passed by on the same highway, nervously eyeing the lightning that nipped the air. An onset of heavy rain muddied signs of the wreck. The dirtbike's broken yellow handguard, jutting from a fringed bush, presented as just a flower. The dismembered foot peg, flat on the blacktop, looked nothing more than mud and soiled leaves.

I would not abandon my saints. With Heaven's roving blessing, I visited them, guiding them in their error with my intently focused eye. Doubling back, the saints arrived at my mark and filed out to reclaim the Boy.

They came upon a site of blood and mire. The road-rash on his naked back was like an ancient script — it held the criss-cross of the tumbleweed, the intertangled canopy of kinfolk trees, the mazeway through Heaven's convolutions. Lying just beyond the bisected front shocks of the bike, the iron chain that bound the Boy and vulture together had severed. Atop a nearby rock, the vulture balanced on its one sound foot. It hissed a greeting at the saints, then throbbed a vomit of a half-devoured field mouse scavenged from the earth.

I sat up in my bed. Eastern gusts swept the windows open, erupting the room in clamor as the old brass hinges sang and the aging wood shutters battered the walls. A humid fog billowed into the room as if animated, as if it would part to reveal Mr. Muir streaking toward me with the sickle.

I lost my sight of the saints as they approached the injured Boy, though their sufferings I paraphrase here as told to me by Mateo, the one who survived:

Upon laying hands on him, the Boy's celestial stature provoked the guardianship of the earth. Lush fields and loblolly pine, grass blades, the wildlands, the earth mire—all gave of its color in an instant, like Heaven flipped the switch from dewy fen to a nightmarish obsidian burn—while the very sphere of the air that surrounded them assumed a pulsing shade of the severest amber.

The Boy sat up.

The heavens above rumbled their displeasure. A colossal suite of nimbostratus clouds skimmed above the search party, spreading east to west over the Texas flatlands as far as any eye could see and dusted them with freezing rain. The bramble covered with hoarfrost. The clouds then shaded through with throbbing golden light—a searing fulmination—as Heaven's judgment streaked earthbound.

When the lightning struck soil, the touch of Heaven coagulated its fury into a glowing ball the size of a millstone. Burning

blue, the sphere seemed enchanted. It
gamboled around like a hound sniffing a
troublesome rat under the floorboards before
bouncing over the body of the promised
Boy and chasing down Daniel, the nearest
fleeing saint. It caught him. Sundered by
this Heavenly firebolt of a butcher, his parts
subsumed in the miasma of the inky soil.

The remaining men with rakes fled back to the labyrinth of
Acacia's thicket, where only Mateo was preserved from the
dangers therein to provide this account of Heaven's vengeance.

Dear Beloved Reader,

This entry concludes my writing in my little books before this present state of assembling my archive.

The events between that entry and now are these:

After the Boy's escape, a cognizance of Heaven's wavering favor settled among the remaining saints of Acacia. I was unable to contain their whisper campaigns. They became like a watching mantis, and I, the marked housefly. I worked tirelessly to explain our dreams—ordered them music and story—threatened punishment that blooms maturation— provided them special ceremony in the chapel. But these were my best seeds thrown to the fire.

I lacked the resources to reclaim the Boy, though I felt certain he had only ventured as far as Clementine. Even as I armed myself with my rake and cloak and ventured into the thicket to track him myself, Heaven neutralized my ambitions and I found only the old blue truck, the inlet, and a return into Acacia.

In order to attain some small victory, I ordered that the damaged orb be repaired. This was acquiesced with precisely the remaining panels of tin the Nightingale had purchased. The handsome prison was renewed as though she knew her child's needs, as though my rebellion had never occurred, though it now lacked its perfect purpose to hold a captive.

Several more apostates slipped away. Not by night, nor with secrecy, but in the sweltering afternoon of a Tuesday. Lacking any preparation, these agents merely agreed to their intent, dropped their rakes and candles, and departed into the thicket. No threat of Heaven's correction would turn their faces back to me. Such is the bent defiance of wayward souls, though I wish now I had followed them at a distance that I might find again the tracks and my train.

Two months after the flight of the Boy, I sensed an impetus. I was to consummate my account.

The urge to write in the early morning was not unusual, as I often rose to meditate in quietude. But on this occasion, I understood I was to greet the dawn not from my bed, but from the top of the orb. To compose from the sum of my maturity, I brought along the totality of my little books written from captive in my sheds to matriarch. I packed them into a leather satchel and wore it across my shoulders. I dressed in my old, soiled overalls for a splash of inspiration. And then I quit my room.

Too early to disturb my saints to labor the staircase to the orb, I parked one of our trucks alongside it. Then, I carried a ladder. From the roof of the cab, I extended it to the orb's steep crest and carefully crawled across the bridge. I then peered into the fathoms of the orb. I could not make out the ground. It appeared bottomless, infinite, and I wished I'd brought a stone to cast in for sound, or the Rapture to plumbline its depths. I turned instead to contemplating the sunrise. Cross-legged in that evident morning peace, the metal warmed beneath me as I sketched the refreshing eye of the sun revealing itself through the pines; a celestial pageant, slow, orange, and menacing. Grand enough to bestow conversion.

Giving in to such majesty, I erred. For I stood, stretching out my arms, and opening my mouth as if to feed, and if my vulture here had swooped, I would have gripped its taloned feet and soared the heavens. But teetering on the roof, my vision dislocated, and I lost balance. A shuffling misstep backward carried me down through the hole, with my satchel, with all my little books, with my pencils, and my canteen, deep into the fathoms of the orb.

That fall was not endless. I did not see the totality of my life on the big screen. I did not have sense of my small, clumsy error, or the tragedy that might claim its end. I did not cry out, or flail my limbs, or feel the seizing terror of weightlessness. I fell as the victim of my causation, serene in the knowledge that from the origin of time, my events had been ordered for such a folly as this.

The impact of earth undid me. The flowers I had planted had long died. Without the Boy to water them, my welcome was parched, unforgiving Acacian dirt.

When my breath returned, I rolled to my knees. I stood, and contemplated, and mustered heart. Soon the saints would wake. As they had so many times before, they'd find me missing. They'd murmur and fret and then gather at the table where they'd form a search party with our best hunters at the lead. They'd then spill from the Pear House and notice the truck backed up to the orb and the ladder stretched to its roof and quickly deduce where their Prophetess had fallen.

For now, however, the grounds were an empty nest. I waited patiently. Meanwhile, I perused my little books, vomiting as I did often in recent times, afterwards wetting my mouth with the canteen.

The sun crested the opening of the orb. It lingered, paused for cruel conversation. And at the creamy yellow of its flare, pangs of dread set in.

For the first time in many years, stillness revealed the sound of a train all around me. It was a raucous passing, sounding with the rhythmic overturn of the rail joints and each shuddering regularity of the movement of so much metal against such a thin brace. I returned to a time in a boxcar with my mates of the rails, who strummed Donovan songs on nylon stringed Spanish guitars and doled out Saltines and Starbursts for their ante at cards. Beneath our bottoms, the steady mechanical churn of our great iron horse. I had pressed my father's luck and won and afterwards drank railway swill while a broke and bare-chinned youth and I fondled each other behind crates of red potatoes. His name was Slow-Down Dennis. We joked about our children.

Rail squeal shocked me back to fact. The sound faded and stillness obtained. My thoughts turned to the end of days.

Would the sound of Heaven's final advent be cataclysm? Having cried out, would the rocks crescend to the ocean? Would froth and flame spill from the mountaintops in agonizingly slow, pining torture, those in exodus swallowed in red? Would the plates of the earth open, welcoming the termagants into legions of swarming worms? Seas whip their contents and drown cities. There is tyranny in every quarter. A screech and the collision of metal and a child cradles the head of his mother's corpse. A sister is slain for a can of tuna. Anything for a swallow of liquor, or to see life afresh, for all one wishes with mortal vision are the edible pink blossoms of an oleander sprouting against so much ash. In a rioted, blown-out building, five bullets remain in Mr. Muir's revolver. A rake of Acacia has traveled many hands. Someone grips it behind a doorway. Sprung mousetraps under the window alert that intruders have breached the haven. Bottle rockets serve as diversion for spent ammunition. Hunters are hunted. All living know their last days. The Acacian rake descends against a raider's head, who seeks only a tablespoon of water.

Or would Heaven's final advent be carried out through the hostility of bourbon-flushed politicians? A prejudice from headquarters shaped to national outrage. The mazework of Acacia revealed to an incursion of GI Joes wearing flak jackets, rappelling from helicopters, lobbing smoke grenades and zinging bullets from automatic rifles as the remaining saints huddle inside the chapel, awaiting flame or despoilment or carnage or captivity like helpless tonsured clergy in a Northman raid.

Or would the sound of Heaven's final advent be silence? Silence like the well-oiled escalator in Fayetteville's department stores. Like an anointed limb noiselessly massaged of its spasm. Like the elysian arbiter had fallen asleep and dreamed instead the peace of a New Year's morning, when the house guests have earned their noontime rousal through so many compliments and such great cheer and the dishes perch so mightily they demand another day. Is Heaven this merciful a lover, sleepy and forgetful, unspeaking when both are spent?

Or would Heaven's final advent be this—our transgressions bloom out of us like helium balloons. There is no longer anything hidden. Nothing buried. No jealous thought of the perfect symmetry of a rival's jaw, no hidden notes between a brother-lover pocketed, no origin story of a Prophetess reshaped for palatable consumption. Mr. Muir sits at the hand of a green John Deere backhoe in his linen suit, joyous in his dig as he plumbs the boneyards of earth and dumps our bodies to the sky. Grotesqueries, we rise like pungent incense. A welcome feast for the golden purifiers circling in the next plane. The vultures nibble on our shames, they glutton on them, and when they are finished, they depart for Heaven. All that remains of us are picked-over bones.

Would Heaven's final advent be swift? This grand experiment of the Divine, Acacia, revealed as a bettor's empty pocket and chalked up as loss. One of many, the next one better. A candle snuffed, all for naught.

Heaven's final advent could be any fashion. I bang the walls of the orb until my palms bleed and the violence of the echoes sends me to my knees. I holler, plead, and threaten with every stripe of my spirit. Oh deliverer, come and save me.

There is no indication a soul remains in Acacia. Not a whisper. No assurance Heaven has carried me in its rapture, in its final advent, whatever shape these Commotions take.

My canteen never diminishes. I feast on my papers and on the flowers I planted for the Boy, now again in bloom. My belly grows with child, and soon, as water springs from the rock, I will give birth to Fontaine Caldwell, the name which Heaven dictates. My brother's—the Boy's—Heaven's—mine is a welcoming womb for one of these truant fathers.

My dear Reader, I have made this book for you of my own wounds and visions. The afterlife of my book, not my own life.

I study the sky, beyond the orb's hole. When the sun crests, I split its center. In the just beyond, I see a citadel in the clouds. I see my vulture's beak. Surely, it tends me.

EAST TEXAS, LATE 1980s. In the eastern part of Texas, nearby the Lake O' The Pines, dawn fog hazes a lumber mill; sifts across the grime of its broken windows and settles over the rotten floorboards. Outside, the shells of rusted gas pumps stand amidst the overwhelm of bramble. A short rake leans against one of the casings. Famined animals chance for a pick at one of their own, bloated and split between the pumps.

Mounted from the roof of the mill, a triangular sign sits on a rusted, candy cane striped pole. Its fossilized neon bulbs are broken. Bullet holes decorate the metal. Prior decades populated this mill. Kept its bustle. But that boom is gone, the mill long fallen to ruination, and the thicket overtakes steadily, soundlessly, at the speed of storms and seasons.

East Texas stillness, broken by the cries of a healthy, squalling girl. A cord binds them, Petra to Fontaine.

Outside, a boy gathers strewn, loose pages, tossed about in the breeze. Vultures perch in nearby branches, atop the roof, on the hood of an old blue truck, craning their blood wine faces for a peer inside the windows. They are quiet like a miracle; like an homage.

Acknowledgments

I wish to thank Suzanne, Selah Saterstrom, Matthew Schmitz, Joanna Howard, Clark Davis, and Sarah Schantz for their exquisite presence and generative conversations throughout the vision and writing of this book; to my editor, PJ Carlisle, and to J. Bruce Fuller, Katie Jean Shinkle, and the staff of TRP—for their attentive eyes and guidance; also to these friends, mentors, and fellow writers for their kindness and influence: Laird Hunt, Brian Kiteley, Janice Lee, W. Scott Howard, Karla Heeps, Jackie Spradley, Carolee Nimmer, Jean-Paul Vessel, Timothy Cleveland, Jenny & Brandon Thunders, Aimee Acorn, Christian Atley, Michael Balusek, Joe Blablazo, Lorenzo Sariñana, Wes Penny, Emily Faulstich, Shae & Brett DeTar, Carly Marie, and The Cave and Edward's for a place to write; also to the DU and Denver writing community, with special thanks to Rowland Rahim Saifi, Mark Meyer, Natalie Rogers, Kelly Krumrie, HR Hegnauer, Jaime Groetsema, Brian Foley, Christopher Rosales, Alicia Wright, and Mairead Case; also thanks to Katie Fallon and Thom van Dooren for their work on vultures. And finally, to my family, my children, and the Fords, always, for their love, grace, presence, and encouragement.

An excerpt of *Acacia, a book of wonders* previously appeared in *Annulet: a Journal of Poetics*.